WITHDRAWN

W9-CAB-504

i so
don't do
makeup

You so don't want to
miss Barrie Summy's
other books!

i so
don't do
mysteries

i so
don't do
spooky

3 1526 03852988 6

i so don't do makeup

Barrie Summy

Delacorte Press

This is a work of fiction. Names, characters, places, and incidents
either are the product of the author's imagination or are used
fictitiously. Any resemblance to actual persons, living or dead, events,
or locales is entirely coincidental.

Copyright © 2010 by Barbara Summy

All rights reserved. Published in the United States by Delacorte Press,
an imprint of Random House Children's Books, a division of Random
House, Inc., New York.

Delacorte Press is a registered trademark and the colophon is a
trademark of Random House, Inc.

Visit us on the Web! www.randomhouse.com

Educators and librarians, for a variety of teaching tools, visit us at
www.randomhouse.com/teachers

Library of Congress Cataloging-in-Publication Data
Summy, Barrie.
I so don't do makeup / Barrie Summy. — 1st ed.
p. cm.
Summary: When Phoenix, Arizona, seventh-grader Sherry Baldwin
hosts a makeover sleepover that causes horrible reactions in her
friends' skin, she enlists the help of her mother, a ghost detective at
the Academy of Spirits, to help solve the mystery of the tainted
makeup.
ISBN 978-0-385-73788-3 (alk. paper)
ISBN 978-0-375-89653-8 (e-book)
[1. Ghosts—Fiction. 2. Mothers and daughters—Fiction.
3. Cosmetics—Fiction. 4. Mystery and detective stories.] I. Title.
II. Title: I so do not do makeup.
PZ7.S9546Iam 2010
[Fic]—dc22
2009028265

The text of this book is set in 12-point Century Schoolbook.

Book design by Marci Senders

Printed in the United States of America
10 9 8 7 6 5 4 3 2 1

First Edition

Random House Children's Books supports the First Amendment
and celebrates the right to read.

For the fam, in ascending order, Claire, Drew, Stephen, Stan and, of course, Mark, who were all very generous about sharing their home and toys with Sherry et al

acknowledgments

In writerly areas . . . thank you to my gifted editor, Wendy Loggia, who makes even revisions fun; my hardworking agent, Rachel Vater, who is always there for me, despite the three-hour time difference; my talented critique partners, Kelly Hayes and Kathy Krevat, who didn't know what they were getting into when we formed Denny's Chicks; and my wonderful and wacky online author group, the late Florence Moyer, Misty Simon, Alli Sinclair, Danita Cahill, Kathy Holmes and Maureen McGowan. Thank you also to Eileen Bagg-Rizzo for special powers in the areas of listening, decision making and careful driving.

And a huge shout-out to the team at Delacorte Press Random House Children's Books for working extra überhard at getting this book in great shape and out into the world in record time: Beverly Horowitz, my publisher; Marci Senders, most creative designer; Heather Lockwood Hughes, ultra-observant copy editor; and Krista Vitola, super organizer.

In other areas, I'd like to thank the following experts: Detective Sergeant Joseph Bulkowski (for police stuff), Reissah Leigh (who knows everything about cosmetics and then some), Dieter Steinmetz (for help with the mysteries of chemistry), Kaveh Shakeri (also for help with chemistry) and Bernard Marcos (*pour l'aide avec le français ainsi que les bons temps à Sherbrooke*). Any errors are all mine.

i so don't do makeup

chapter
one

I slip into the bathroom next to my bedroom and stand quietly on the cool tile floor. Looking around, I breathe out a sigh of happiness.

Lined up on the counter are bottles and jars and tubes and adorable little pots. Of powders and liquids and gels and sprays. Next to brushes and wands and cotton balls and small sponge wedges. All brand-new. All unopened. All beautiful.

I, Sherry (short for Sherlock) Holmes Baldwin, am hosting the makeup slumber party of the century.

The doorbell rings.

Taking two at a time, I bound down the stairs and yank open the front door.

Brianna, my overly chatty, overly boy-crazy, overly

dramatic friend, squeals. She springs into our foyer, drops her pink sleeping bag, her flowered pillow and her paisley backpack and hugs me. "You throw the best sleepovers!"

After Brianna releases me, I take a step back. I tip my head to the side, make a rectangular shape with my hands, and regard her face through my fingers. I so cannot wait to break out the blusher.

"What're you doing?" Brianna asks.

"I got this magazine that's full of cool makeup tips," I say, "like how to glamorize your eyes and groom your brows and determine your face shape."

"Face shape?" she says. "What's mine?"

"I haven't actually read the whole article yet, but whatever you are, it'll be good. We can deal with every shape."

"Sherry, this is going to rock."

We're halfway up the stairs when the doorbell chimes again. I jog back down while Brianna heads to my room to stash her gear.

I fling open the door. "Hi, Kim!"

Kim stands on the stoop, her elbows straight and stiff, a blue pillow under one arm, a blue sleeping bag under the other. Her fingers curl around the handle of an overnight bag on wheels, which stands upright and well behaved beside her. "Hi, Sherry."

I'm not really sure why Kim agreed to come this

evening. She doesn't wear makeup at all. As in *not at all.*

Kim belongs to the Janes, a bizarro group of girls at school who refuse to use cosmetics. Personally, I don't get it. There are loads of other things in life I'd give up first. Like carrots. Or homework. Even chocolate.

I invited Kim because we're doing a French project together and because she's Josh's cousin. When you're dating Josh Morton, the coolest, cutest eighth grader in Phoenix, Arizona, you sort of get sucked into his family.

But honestly? I thought Kim would say no.

There's a short knock at the door and then it swings slowly open. My BFF, Junie Carter, slides her solid black backpack, her glow-in-the-dark-constellations sleeping bag and her plain white pillow across the entrance tiles and into a corner. She hands me a plastic grocery bag of lumpiness. "From my mom."

I peek inside. Snacks! "Yay, Junie." I pull out a tub of sour gummy worms.

She smiles, then glances around and continues in a low voice, "My mom was worried The Ruler wouldn't have enough junk food to last us the night."

Totally legit worry. The Ruler, my stepmother, is a bona fide health-food granola bar. She's nicknamed The Ruler for two reasons. Her posture is insanely straight, like she's a human ruler. And she teaches math at my middle school, where she's definitely the strictest teacher. Don't even think about handing in your homework late.

My real mother would've been good for endless junk food. She was an awesome cop with the Phoenix Police Department who died about two years ago during a drug bust gone bad. Now she's a ghost detective with the Academy of Spirits, an organization dedicated to watching over humans and keeping us safe. The cool thing is that, although I can't see her, I can talk to her. We even solve mysteries together for the Academy.

Weirdly, my grandfather is also an Academy member, but in a mascotty way. After his humongous heart attack, Grandpa chose to become a cactus wren, our state bird. He spends a load of time hanging out at Grandma's, in the hopes she'll recognize him.

I pop open the candy container and offer it to Kim.

"Sour gummies are my weakness," she says, scooping up a handful.

Phew. I wasn't really sure if the Janes enforced sugar rules too.

"You'll be happy, then," Junie says. "There's enough in the bag for the entire seventh grade."

The Ruler walks down the hall from the kitchen.

"Hi, Ms. Paulson," Junie and Kim say, automatically straightening their shoulders.

4

The Ruler married my dad a few months ago but didn't change her name at school. "I already ordered the pizza," she says to me.

Junie's eyes go big behind her glasses. I know exactly what she's thinking. The Ruler? Pizza? Will it be whole wheat with soy cheese?

With my thumb and index finger, I give my stepmother an okay sign.

As we're tramping upstairs, Junie pokes me in the back. "Pizza?"

"Olives, anchovies and fat-free organic goat cheese," I say with a straight face.

"Ewww!" Junie and Kim say together.

"Kidding." I grin. "It's pepperoni from Angelo's. She really wants us to have a good time," I say. "She even sent Sam to Grandma Baldwin's." I look over my shoulder at Kim. "You're allowed pizza, right?"

She rolls her eyes. "Duh."

"Kim, I gotta show you my bedroom," I say, walking through the open door. "I mixed two different paints to get the wall color. Turquoise and sea green. And I hot-glue-gunned all those fake gemstones around the door and across the windowsill."

"Very cool." Kim gazes around. "What kind of fish are those?"

"Bala sharks." Anyone who notices my fish can't be too difficult. Maybe she's going to fit in after all. Maybe my makeover slumber party will be what

5

convinces Kim to quit the Janes and join the world of normal girls at Saguaro Middle School.

Brianna's in the bathroom, ogling the cosmetics array. Bright red spots of excitement dot her cheeks. I'll go easy on the blush for her. "Sherry, where'd all this come from?"

Kim peeks in the bathroom and gulps. The way I gulp right before a big test.

I hand her the tub of gummy worms. "Mostly from Naked Makeup."

"Did Amber help you?" Junie asks.

"Yeah." Amber, Junie's gorgeous but often obnoxious cousin is in high school and knows everything about makeup and boys and life. About a month ago, Amber started working part-time at Naked Makeup, this new kiosk in the mall. Naked Makeup's products are natural and healthy and not tested on animals. The best part is you get to choose from a variety of scents and glitters and they customize the cosmetics for you.

Junie recently tiptoed into the world of makeup. And guys. Before that, she concentrated on school and getting all As. She's an only child with two high-IQ engineer parents.

I unscrew the lid from a pot of lip gloss. "The Ruler agreed to help pay for the makeup if we went with botanical products. And Amber offered me her employee discount if I bought more than five items."

"Wow," Brianna says. "Wow. Wow."

Kim's jaw is chomping up and down on the gummies.

Junie's picking up bottles and reading the ingredients.

"I will so get a boyfriend with all this makeup on," Brianna says.

"I love how you can choose your own flavor." I hold out the lip gloss. "Smell this, guys. It's cookie dough."

Brianna grabs the pot.

Kim shoves another gummy worm in her mouth.

Junie sticks in her slightly-too-long-but-which-I-will-fix-with-shading nose. "It really *does.*"

Brianna takes a humongously noisy whiff. She pokes in her index finger and slathers a bunch on her lips. Outside the lines.

The Ruler calls from the bottom of the stairs, "Girls, pizza's here!"

We power to the kitchen, where we grab barstools. The Ruler has plates and cups and a jug of something juice-ish set out for us.

So we're all comfy and sitting there and friendly. Just chatting about classes and homework and movies. Kim's starting to warm up.

Brianna drops her slice of pizza on her plate and stares at Kim. "There's something I've been wanting to ask you for forever." She leans on her elbows.

7

"Why do you guys call yourselves the Janes? There's not even a Jane in your group."

Trust Brianna to ask the hard-hitting questions. That girl will say absolutely anything. Also, she is not known for her secret-keeping skills. Do not tell her if you're crushing on a guy and you don't want him to know. I speak from experience.

Kim gives a weak smile. "Well, you know, like, plain Jane. Simple and real."

"Which also means drab and uninteresting." Junie is a human thesaurus.

Kim crosses her arms. "Studies have shown that girls who don't wear makeup in middle school get higher grades in math and science. And girls who get higher grades in math and science graduate from good colleges and land professional jobs." She's a walking, talking brochure.

"Why can't you have it all?" I reach for a second slice of pizza.

"What do you mean?" Kim asks.

"I mean why can't you look great *and* get good grades?" I stare at Kim right in her unadorned eyes. "You could be the first Jane to break out of the mold. You could wear makeup and look gorgeous and have a boyfriend and get great grades and become whatever professional it is you want to be."

"Seriously, be a Glam Pam," Brianna says. "Glam

Pam. I like that. I made up that rhyme this very second."

Kim frowns.

I can't help but notice her eyebrows are begging for a date with a pair of tweezers.

"Or maybe a Break-the-Chains Jane," Junie says.

Kim nods a fraction of a nod.

"Actually, what are you doing here?" Brianna asks.

"My aunt talked me into it." Kim shakes her head like maybe it wasn't the best suggestion. "She said I'm still pretty new to Saguaro and I need to keep meeting people."

Kim's aunt Vicki—aka Josh's mom—is a hairdresser with the best highlights, high heels and fake nails. She's super gabby and super smart about girl stuff. I'm guessing Vicki knows all about the Janes and is counting on me to turn Kim around.

We finish eating without any more awkward questions from Brianna. Then it's back upstairs for Naked Makeup time! Junie, Brianna and I bounce up the stairs. Kim lags.

"I'm first," Brianna announces, pulling the chair from my bedroom into the bathroom.

I drape a bath towel across Brianna, pull her hair back in a ponytail and sponge her face with a warm wet washcloth. Then, exactly like a surgeon performing delicate surgery, I start calling out for stuff.

"Cleanser," I announce.

Junie places it in my waiting palm.

"Astringent. Toner. Towel. Bronzer."

During all this, Kim's hanging by the bathroom door, nervous and twitchy, ready to make a break for it if we get too close with a makeup brush.

"Before we start slapping on makeup, we gotta figure out our face shapes." I open my magazine and smooth it flat on the counter. Then I uncurl a measuring tape. "Who wants to go first?"

"Me, me, me." Brianna waves her arm in the air.

Such an enthusiastic subject! I measure across her jawline, across her cheekbones, across the widest part of her forehead and from her hairline down to her chin.

"This is so exciting, Sherry." Brianna talks without moving her lips, like a ventriloquist.

I jot down the numbers on a Post-it note, then stick it to the page with all the face shape info.

Brianna leans over, her hair brushing the page, muttering her numbers under her breath. "Same width at forehead and cheekbones. Narrow chin." Her finger pauses on one of the shapes and taps. "Oblong?" she wails. "I'm oblong? It says oblong is the worst shape!"

"I bet lots of movie stars have oblong faces," Junie says.

"How would you know?" Brianna pushes up on her chin. "You only watch the Science Channel."

"Bri, it's like I told you before," I say. "All face shapes can be beautiful. We'll work with you, especially in the shading department. And you could think about getting a haircut." I look closer at the article. "It says to avoid long straight hair, like yours, with an oblong face."

"Oblong," Brianna repeats. "This explains so much of what's gone wrong in my life."

Junie's reading the magazine page, the tip of her tongue poking out between her front teeth. A sure sign of concentration for her. "So, I'm round. And I should grow my hair down past my chin and get rid of the frizziness, especially by my ears."

"Sounds right to me." I give her a thumbs-up.

"And you're a heart." Junie draws the shape in the air.

"Great," I say sarcastically. "I've always wanted a pointy chin."

Of course, Kim has the perfect face. Oval.

I drag my desk chair into the bathroom. "Have a seat, Junie." I flap a towel, then drape it over her. I unscrew a bottle and drip some of its contents on a cotton pad. "Freckle Fade."

Junie plunks herself down in the chair faster than you can say Pippi Longstocking. She's always been unhappy with her freckles. And her red hair.

I start dabbing. "Amber said the solution in Freckle Fade isn't bleach. So, while somewhat drying, it

11

won't totally suck the moisture from your skin and leave you looking like a raisin."

"Sounds good," Junie says through parted lips.

"What about your eyebrows?" Brianna asks.

It's a delicate subject because Junie's eyebrows are unruly and forestlike.

Junie's hands pop up from under the towel and she smacks them over her brows. "Don't touch them. I'm not up for that much pain."

I can see her point.

While Junie's fading, I start on Brianna, using as many products as possible. I'm especially generous with the blemish concealer. With a large flat brush, I paint blush strokes on an upward angle over Brianna's cheekbones to minimize her facial length. Junie dusts her with bronzer.

The result: amazing.

Even Kim, who's sitting on my bed, notices a difference.

With lots of instruction from me, Brianna does my face. Junie watches closely.

Eventually the three of us are made up and beautiful.

I call Kim into the bathroom. "Look in the mirror, Kim," I say. "You've got the most perfect cheekbones."

"And you're an oval," Brianna says admiringly.

"How about a light dusting of blush?" I wave the brush in the air. "I'm talking überlight."

"Okay," she says.

I think Kim's more interested in makeup than she's admitting.

The next part of the slumber party is all about sprawling in the family room, munching on junk food and watching movies.

Late, late at night, exhausted and bleary-eyed, we roll out our sleeping bags, then trudge into the bathroom to brush our teeth.

"One more thing, guys." I yawn. "Night cream."

"Enough with the makeup." Brianna yawns back at me and the fluorescent light bounces off her braces. That girl can be very cranky when tired.

"Amber promised if we leave the Nite Sprite Creme on overnight, we won't even recognize our own skin. It'll glow and sparkle and shimmer," I say. "It's got magic mini moisturizing beads."

Junie picks up the Nite Sprite Creme bottle. "The beads are filled with vitamin E and dissolve over several hours."

"We'll totally own Saguaro Middle School come Monday morning," I say.

Propped up against the bathroom wall, Brianna nods sleepily.

We wash off our makeup, then smear thick peach-colored unscented cream from our necks to our foreheads. Total coverage. I hit Junie extra hard because of the Freckle Fade. Only her tiny brown eyes squint out from a sea of orange. Kim steadfastly refuses to join in. Which just goes to show how stubborn a Jane can be.

I'm already snuggled in my sleeping bag and halfway to dreamland when Junie says, "My face is tingling. Are you sure this stuff is okay, Sherry?"

"I'm sure. It's from Amber," I mumble into the dark. "Go to sleep." I roll over. "Suck it up for beauty."

"Yeah, but is your face tingling?" Junie asks. "Brianna, how about you? How's your face feel?"

Brianna gives a little nasally snort. She zonks out fast.

"Be quiet," Kim complains.

Three of us dream of beauty and baby-soft skin. One of us dreams of plainness and a business degree.

chapter
two

High-pitched screams rudely rip me from the middle of a delightful dream where Josh and I both have unlimited texting. When I enter the conscious world, I'm tapping <b rite bk> on my thigh.

More screams. From the bathroom. It's Junie.

Brianna, Kim and I catapult out of bed, fly over my sea green + turquoise carpet and onto tile. Because Junie screaming? This. Is. Serious.

Is there a diamondback rattlesnake hissing toward my BFF? Or horror-movie blood dripping down the wall? Or her worst nightmare—a busted calculator?

Junie screams again.

The three of us sprint to her.

No rattlesnake. No blood. No calculator.

Her back toward us, her striped pajamas all wrinkled, Junie turns around and removes her hands from her face.

"Ahhhhh!" I scream.

"Ahhhhh!" Brianna screams.

"Is that from the night cream?" Kim asks.

In slow, slogging-through-Jell-O motion, Brianna and I turn to each other. Her face is blotchy and cracked like the dried-out Arizona desert floor. Her mouth forms a horrified O, and she points at my cheeks.

Suddenly, my face is sizzling. I switch into high gear, cranking the faucet on full blast. Maybe cold water will soothe our ravaged skin. Brianna and I flood our faces like the Hoover Dam's cascading over us. My eyes closed, I reach blindly into the vanity drawer and pull out a couple of washcloths. I wave one in Brianna's general direction. Our flapping hands meet. We blot our faces and, hearts pounding, stare into the mirror.

"Ahhhhh!" I scream.

"Ahhhhh!" Brianna screams.

"It's definitely the night cream," Kim says. Somewhat smugly.

Shoulder to shoulder, Junie, Brianna and I lean

into the mirror. And stare in shock at our red, scaly, peeling skin. Überugly. Poor Junie is the überugliest of all.

"What's going on, girls?" The Ruler's feet scurry along the hall. She pops her head into the bathroom and ogles us. "Oh my."

We turn our sad puffy faces toward her like three little sunflowers in search of the sun. Well, more like three homely lizards.

The Ruler inhales sharply. She glances at the cosmetics on the counter. "Which product did this?"

I hand her the bottle of Nite Sprite Creme.

She skims the ingredients. "Papaya acid is the only abrasive ingredient. But there's so little of it. . . ." She morphs directly into fix-it mode. "Let's try a gentle, nonperfumed hydrating lotion. And something for the swelling." She blasts outta the bathroom.

The Ruler's perfect to have around in crisis situations. She's calm, cool and collected. Plus she's big on never running out of supplies like Band-Aids and Tylenol and real-fruit Popsicles.

"Why do I let you talk me into stuff?" Junie moans to me.

"Your freckles are definitely faded," I say.

Junie's staring into the mirror and grimacing. "Be quiet, Sherry."

Brianna brushes her hair forward over her face. Completely.

I gently prod my chin. It feels tight, like a stretched rubber band. "This is so bad. I'm supposed to meet up with Josh later this aft," I say. "There's no way I'm gonna let him see my face."

Brianna peers out between strands of hair. "Try this." She lurches around the bathroom. "I can actually see better than you think." After crashing into the toilet a couple of times, she parts her hair with her fingers to make bigger eyeholes.

"I don't know, Bri . . . ," I say.

"That look suits you, Brianna," Kim says.

I glare at her and she flounces back to my bedroom.

"You're worried about not seeing Josh?" Junie's voice screeches like the parrots at the zoo. "I could be permanently disfigured. Permanently. As in, forever!" Her pitch soars on "forever," nearing a level called hysterical. "While *you* might have to put off a date for a day?" Her eyes are wild and crazed. "Look at this." She gently clamps her index finger and thumb on a piece of loose skin and it flakes off.

No doubt about it, Junie's face was much harder hit than mine or Brianna's.

The Ruler zips back with four bags of frozen organic peas and a tube of something. She hands a bag of peas each to me and Brianna and two to Junie. "We need to get a leg up on the swelling. Hold these bags against your face, girls, for about fifteen minutes." She waves the tube at us before setting it on the counter. "Then liberally apply this zinc ointment. It's full of vitamins A and E and will really help with skin cell repair. I'll make some green tea for you." She pauses, thinking, her forehead scrunched up. "With a little burdock and aniseed in it." She heads to the kitchen to brew up the curing concoction.

In my bedroom, Junie, Brianna and I drop to the floor. Lying on our backs, we balance the frozen peas on our faces.

I close my eyes and lie there, going numb. Every once in a while, I move the peas from my left cheek to the right to my forehead to my chin. I'm an equal opportunity patient.

Junie set her phone alarm and when it beeps, I pop up, peas sliding to the carpet. "Cream time." My frozen face has trouble forming the words.

Back in the bathroom, we dry off. I unscrew the tube and squirt out a white dollop on Brianna's hand. An herbalish scent fills the small area.

"P.U." Brianna wrinkles her Rudolph nose. "That's disgusting."

Any other time, I would agree, but today herbal smells like healing.

"Give me that." Junie grabs the tube and squeezes out a mountain into her palm.

"You guys look rough." Kim leans against the

bathroom door frame and stares at us with her perfectly oval, milky-skinned face.

She's feeling pretty superior about being a Jane.

"I'm starving." Kim clamps a hand on her hip. "What's for breakfast?"

We don't even bother answering, but rub the thick ointment into our pores.

Her face all greased up and ghostlike, Junie pushes past Kim and grabs her phone from where it's lying by her pillow. Thumbs dancing over the keypad, she says, "I'm Googling 'food and skin rejuvenation.'"

Brianna and I crowd around the tiny phone screen.

"I don't know what silica is or what it has to do with skin repair, but it's in celery and leeks and we have those." I keep reading as Junie scrolls.

Kim's still hanging out by the bathroom door, watching us and shaking her head. "See why I don't wear makeup?"

"It wasn't *makeup*," I say. "It was night cream!"

"Oh look"—Brianna points at the screen—"all this stuff's good for our nails too." She flutters her hands in the air. "Hey, I got these new nail gems, and longer nails would so show them off."

Brianna's not the most focused. Pretty much every sparkly object catches her eye.

"How about something from the zinc category?"

Junie asks. "To work in conjunction with this cream."

Kim rolls up her sleeping bag, then goes into the bathroom. She returns with her toothbrush and toothpaste, which she shoves in her suitcase.

"I'm thinking eggs, pumpkin seeds and a can of salmon." Junie clicks from website to website.

"I don't think you guys can get normal by school tomorrow," Kim says. She pulls up the handle of her suitcase and scoops up her sleeping bag. "My mom's on her way." She exits my bedroom.

Brianna peeps out from behind her hair. "She's gonna open her big fat mouth about this before we even get to our lockers Monday morning." She drops her hair back into place. "You should never've invited her."

"Don't worry," I say. "It won't happen again."

"Leave me off your guest list next time too," Brianna mutters.

I'm beginning to think Brianna is a fair-skinned friend. A little blotchiness and she's all snappy and sarcastic.

As Junie, Brianna and I depart for the kitchen and a bizarro super-skin-repair brunch, I gaze longingly at my lovely bala sharks.

Cindy and Prince are zipping around their tank, little flecks of silver glinting off their tails. No unsightly scales or unpleasant puffiness. Basically no fishy cares or worries other than deciding who's it for aquarium hide-and-seek and waiting for me to sprinkle down the next meal.

I wish I could dive in there and join them.

In the kitchen, my dad says, "Hi, girls," from deep in his newspaper, then folds it up and shuffles out. His eyes are down the whole time, which makes me think The Ruler told him about our facial incident. Girl stuff embarrasses him to the max.

The Ruler emerges from the pantry, a stack of napkins in her hand. "Sherry, can you girls get your own breakfast? There are fresh bagels on the counter. Your dad and I are going over to your grandmother's to pick up Sam."

"Sure thing." I squeeze past her to nab pumpkin seeds and a can of salmon. Not a tasty combo, but it is skin-repair food.

"How does the zinc ointment feel?" she asks.

"Soothing," Junie says. "I just hope it does the trick. Fast."

Brianna's phone buzzes. She flips it open to read the text. "My dad's coming in five. I gotta babysit my sister." She makes a face at the food choices piling up on the counter. "I'm okay with eating at home." She races upstairs to grab her stuff. A few minutes later, she shouts, "Sherry, tell The Ruler thanks." The front door slams.

Junie turns her reddish-whitish face to me. "We should text Amber. I wonder if this has happened before with Nite Sprite Creme."

"Go ahead."

Amber isn't always as nice to us as she could be. Let's just say she's four years older but light-years ahead of us in social stuff. We're like grit in her shoe.

"It should definitely be you." Junie pushes her glasses up her ravaged nose. "This was *your* makeup party. And *you* bought the product off her. And *you're* the one she gave the instructions to. And I've used up all my texts for the month. And—"

I roll my eyes. "Fine."

Junie scoots her barstool close to mine.

I pull out my cell.

<sumthng went wrong with nite sprite creme>

Amber texts back, <no way. naked makeup is all botanical. u didnt follow my instructions>

<we did>

Amber doesn't even dignify my last text with a response.

<ur COUSINS face is way bad. mine isnt gr8>

<im @ work. lemme c>

"No!" Junie says. "I can't go out in public."

"Me either."

"I *really* can't, Sherry."

I type, <we cant come 2 the mall. 2 public>

23

Junie and I both flop forward on the counter and blow out air.

"We're going to the mall," we say at the exact same time.

chapter
three

Plugging her nose, Junie downs the rest of her green tea. She scoops up a handful of pumpkin seeds. "Let's get this over with."

I text The Ruler our plans. Then Junie and I each wrap a pastel-colored scarf around our head. I grab my insanely fashionable new denim purse and drop in the jar of Nite Sprite Creme. Next, we're hoofing it over to the mall. I love living close to shopping.

Without discussion, because that's how BFFs work, we circle around to the back of the building and sneak in via the least busy entrance. We barrel past the vacant, out-of-business shoe store and the under-construction vitamin store. It's easy to avoid eye contact with the guy at the hot-sauce kiosk because he's all engrossed in scrubbing his counter. The scarves are our magic invisible cloaks, and we get all the way to the Naked Makeup kiosk without anyone noticing us.

The kiosk is next to the food court. Which means it's a bopping, bustling, happening kind of place. The beige awning is adorably decorated with pink and purple tissue butterflies. All sorts of containers are perfectly arranged on the counter and along shelves on both sides of the kiosk. At one end, there's a cash register with a vase of fresh-cut colorful flowers. The other end has nail polishes and lipsticks.

With a Q-tip, Amber's painting stripes of different lipstick colors on the back of an old lady's hand. It's one of the wrinkled, blue-haired women who ride the bus out to the Indian casino for bingo. She and her friends followed Amber to Naked Makeup from her previous part-time job at the cosmetics counter in the mall's department store.

Junie approaches her cousin. "Excuse me, Amber."

Amber startles and squeals. She was so focused on her customer that an earthquake could've shaken open a big hole next to the kiosk, sucked her in and spat her out on the other side of the mall, and she wouldn't have noticed. Because that's how Amber does makeup. With all her heart and soul. Lacey, Amber's boss, is the same way.

"Edna and I are busy," Amber says with only a

cursory glance at us. "I'll check with you two when we're done."

Edna holds up her hand, turning it this way and that. "I don't know, dear, what do you think?"

Amber touches the second stripe. "Rose. Definitely. Totally complements your complexion."

Finally, Edna wanders off, clutching a paper shopping bag filled with Naked Makeup merchandise.

"Take off the scarves," Amber says. She never wastes too much time on niceties with Junie and me. Actually, she never wastes any time on them with us.

Hands on hips, Amber gets up close and personal, all the while frowning at our faces, but especially at Junie's. This says something because Amber is usually very aware of potential frown lines. Generally, she keeps her face smooth like Saran Wrap.

From a pocket in her pink + purple butterfly smock, Amber pulls out a magnifying glass. Her eyeball practically glued to it and her head twisting off to the side, she examines Junie's forehead. "What else did you use on her besides Nite Sprite Creme?" she asks me.

"Just that freckle-fading stuff," I say, "which you said was safe."

"It is." Amber slides the magnifying glass back in her pocket. "The fading ingredient is from the root of the paper mulberry tree. It's not at all irritating to the skin."

27

"I slathered the Nite Sprite Creme on really thick," Junie says. And she's such a good friend that she doesn't mention how that was my idea.

Amber nods and taps a finger on her chin. "Lacey'll be back from her break in a few. I want to check with her before recommending anything." She points a long varnished nail to a nearby bench. "Wait over there."

Junie's been kicking it down low, staying out of sight at the back of the kiosk. At Amber's orders, her eyes open wide and panicked. "The bench's right in the path of the American Potato Company. Where every kid from school goes. Someone I know will see me."

"Get a grip, Junie." Amber fluffs her hair. "It's only a matter of time before that happens. We're cosmeticians, not magicians."

Junie stares at the linoleum, her toe grazing the surface. A tear pools in the corner of her eye.

"I'll stand in front of you," I say, taking her arm.

She sniffs. "Thanks, Sherry."

Amber switches on her salesgirl charm and sashays to the other side of the kiosk to help a couple of girls who are oohing and aahing over lip gloss.

Arm in arm, Junie and I shuffle to the bench. She plops down and slouches. I stay on my feet, shielding her from the passersby. We each drape a scarf loosely around our head.

"Lacey's gotta have a magic fix." Junie's voice is all choked up. "I can't go to school tomorrow looking like a freak. But I can't *not* go to school."

Maintaining a 4.0 can really complicate your life. Personally, I'm fine with missing school. Except for not seeing my friends. Although with The Ruler, to stay home you have to prove you're practically dead.

I've been hiding Junie from public view for about five minutes when I see Lacey leaving the food court in teeny-tiny steps. She's wearing the cutest open-toed high heels in history. She's got on the same smock as Amber, and the shoes match the lavender perfectly.

At twenty-four, Lacey's an older, plumper, shorter version of Amber. They both have straight, shoulder-length blond hair and large sparkly eyes fringed with

l gives a friendly wave.
gnizes us.
utes before Lacey and
mers and beckon us over.
ling Lacey in on the Nite

t. I catch a flowery whiff
're in pretty good shape,
finger, she gently prods my
st spent too much time in

29

the sun. Which I know you didn't, but that's as bad as it looks. You'll clear up quickly."

"Thanks," I say. Yay for me. But I feel for Junie. I open my purse and start rooting around in it for the jar of cream. This is the biggest purse I've ever owned, and I could probably lose my brother in it.

In the meantime, Lacey's examining Junie, gingerly touching her cheeks, then her nose. Lacey straightens. "Looks like a chemical peel gone bad. As in, too much acid." She turns to Amber.

"That's exactly what I was thinking." Amber shakes her head and her hair tiptoes across her shoulders.

"There's only two percent papaya acid in Nite Sprite Creme, but this looks like you've been exposed to way more than that." Lacey picks up a bottle of water and unscrews the cap. "How did it feel during the night?"

"Tingly," Junie says. "But then I fell asleep. I woke up this morning because my face was on fire."

"I do throw a pretty intense slumber party," I say. "So once we crash, we're totally out of it."

"The combo of Freckle Fade and the small amount of papaya acid in Nite Sprite could cause a tingling sensation." Lacey squints, thinking. "But I don't see how it would cause burning."

"Should we give them Chockfull O' Nutrients?" Amber holds up a purple jar.

"Definitely." Lacey sips some water. "Chockfull's got organic jojoba oil, which is like sebum, the oil your own skin produces," she says to Junie and me. "It's also got ground-up carob seeds to exfoliate the damaged skin and help with skin repair."

"We better take some for our friend Brianna," I say. "She was at my party too, and her skin looks like mine."

Lacey tips Junie's chin and frowns. "Junie, I guess somehow the combo of Nite Sprite Creme and Freckle Fade and the fact that you put the Nite Sprite Creme on super thick . . ." She screws the cap back on her water. "I don't get it, though. I only opened Naked Makeup a few months ago, but we haven't had problems with any of our products. And we sell a ton of Nite Sprite."

Amber flips through a little calendar next to the cash register. "I sold to Sherry on Thursday. That same day I filled a few individual bottles with Nite Sprite Creme to finish off the batch."

"We haven't had any complaints about the other bottles from that batch," Lacey says.

"And I followed our protocol and didn't add a fragrance," Amber says.

Lacey opens a cupboard at the bottom of the kiosk and pulls out a white plastic container the size of a gallon jug of milk. She twists off the top and scoops out lotion with her baby finger. She sniffs it, then

31

smears a little on the inside of her wrist. "This is the new batch of Nite Sprite Creme. I'll leave it on to see if I get a reaction. I can tell you right now, I'm feeling nothing."

Finally, my fingers bump up against the Nite Sprite Creme at the bottom of my purse. I set it on the counter. "Here's my jar."

Lacey opens it, smells the contents, then dabs some on her wrist. "Smells like Nite Sprite." She passes the jar to Amber, who glances in it, then shrugs.

"How long will I look like this?" Junie's scaly forehead is etched with worry lines.

"A few days, I'm guessing," Lacey says. "However, along with the Chockfull O' Nutrients cream, I'll give you this superhydrating spray. It's mostly for elderly skin, but it'll help so you don't feel so tight and dry."

"I don't care how I feel," Junie says, "I care how I look."

Wow. Junie has come a long way socially. I give her a hug.

Lacey busies herself with pulling out papers and reading about Nite Sprite and Chockfull O' Nutrients.

"Lacey, your wrist!" Amber says.

Sure enough, there's an angry red circle where she applied my cream.

"I'm sending this in to corporate for testing." Lacey yanks a wipe from a dispenser on the counter.

"Customers." Amber gestures with her head to a group of older teens who're congregating on the other side of the kiosk. She hands us the samples Lacey mentioned, then sends us her patented "get lost" look. It's true that we're not very good advertising.

"Amber, you handle the customers." Lacey rolls the stool by the register and motions to Junie to sit. "I wanna work with Junie for a minute."

Flicking her hair over a shoulder, Amber flounces off.

Junie sinks onto the stool. "Thank you."

I'm staring into a magnifying mirror hanging on the kiosk, massaging in Chockfull O' Nutrients and commenting to Junie and Lacey on the silkiness of the cream and how I can practically see an immediate improvement. Seriously, I'm looking ready for some prime time with Josh.

When coincidence of coincidences, my phone sings out "You're the One," by the Boyfriends.

It's my boy!

chapter
four

I flip open my phone.

"Hey, Sherry."

At the sound of my cute, wonderful eighth-grade boyfriend's perfect voice, a shiver skitters up and down my spine. I could melt at the way he shushes out the *sh*, glides over the *e*, whirs over the *r*'s, then hangs out on the *y*.

"Hi, Josh. Whatcha doing?"

"I'm at the mall."

"Seriously?" I mouth to Junie, *He's here!* Then I point to my face, my eyebrows up and questioning.

You're fine, Junie mouths back. With both index fingers, she points to her own face. *Not like me!*

"What are you doing at the mall?" I ask Josh while

staring at myself in the mirror. Do I *really* look close enough to normal for a boyfriend encounter?

"Sherry," Lacey says, "I'll touch up your makeup when I'm done with Junie."

I mouth *Okay.*

"Nick and I are here doing recon," Josh says. "Trying to figure out who to interview for our video."

"You're with Nick?" I'm watching Junie as I repeat the info.

She gets a wild-eyed, caged-animal look.

"Are you and Junie free? Wanna meet us at Jazzed-Up Juice?"

"Uh, oops, I have another call coming in. Uh, it's The Ruler. And you know I have to answer those. I'll call you right back. Bye." I snap my phone shut. "Junie, they want to meet at Jazzed-Up Juice."

Junie looks like she's gonna throw up.

"What should I say?"

"No!" she screeches. "Say no!"

"Hold still." Lacey's got a glob of foundation on a sponge wedge.

"You can't avoid Nick forever," I say. "Can you keep your head turned or something, and I'll block you?"

Junie sighs.

"China clay is the best concealer ever invented." Lacey sponges Junie's cheeks, forehead, nose and chin. Then, with the pads of her fingers, she quickly pats the concealer on evenly. "I swear it could cover

35

cracks in a sidewalk." Next, with a huge brush, she dusts on powder. "Cool, huh?" Lacey says, stepping back to admire her handiwork.

"It's incredible!" I say. It's not a miracle, but it's a massive improvement.

Junie makes faces in the mirror, checking out how she looks with a frown, a smile, her eyebrows raised, her head turned. "I do look less, uh, damaged."

"So?" My eyebrows and shoulders jump up in a question.

"Yes, we'll hit Jazzed-Up Juice."

I text Josh to say we'll be there in five, then switch spots with Junie. Lacey gives me the same makeup treatment. When she's done, I say, "A million thank-yous." Because I look fantastic. Truly.

Then, arm in arm, Junie and I skip down the aisle to Jazzed-Up Juice. Well, more like I'm skipping and dragging while she's shuffling. Partly I'm skipping because I'm looking A1. Partly I'm skipping because I'm meeting Josh. If I were meeting Nick, I'd be shuffling too.

Nick and I just don't click. He's always giving me a hard time. Which, of course, I so don't deserve.

Skip, skip, skip. Drag, drag, drag. Shuffle, shuffle, shuffle. Past Brittani's Baubles and Movie World and the amazing Sequins, where I will one day buy my prom dress.

"I'm so torn, Sherry." Junie tightens her grip on

my arm to slow me down. "I'm excited about seeing Nick, but at the same time, I don't want to see him at all because of my face."

"Love *is* strange." I can say this with experience. Josh and I have been an item for over three months.

Junie and I are jaunting along at a steady pace, when into my brain leaps a creative thought about my BFF. "Junie, we could easily direct attention away from your skin and in a beautiful, colorful way." I stop skipping, drop Junie's arm and start scrounging around in my purse.

Junie halts mid-shuffle and regards me. Warily.

It takes a few minutes to find what I'm looking for because in some ways, my purse resembles a black hole. But eventually, I pull out a small, rectangular plastic container. "Thickly applied eye shadow!" I point toward the restrooms. "We can zip in here, and I'll brush your lids with a couple of coats of navy and dark gray."

Junie grabs my elbow and motors me away from the restroom entrance, spitting out a word with each step. "Sherry, I am not ever taking any chances with you and makeup and my face again in this lifetime. Ever."

Humph. We jaunt along in silence after that. Probably Junie is feeling sorry about her unkind remark to me. The makeup incident was not my fault!

Josh and Nick are waiting for us at Jazzed-Up

Juice, where they scored a table and four plastic chairs. Josh spots me and holds up a cup. He waves us over, pointing to the middle of the table, where the drink he already bought me sits. No doubt it's Strawberry Swirl, my fave. The boy knows my taste.

Nick pushes back his chair and stands when we get close. He kind of stares at Junie's face, but, thankfully, has a moment of social smartness and doesn't blurt out something stupid and tactless. "Junie, what juice strikes your fancy?"

Strikes your fancy? Seriously, dude, talk middle-school English.

Junie, however, giggles at his question. The two of them amble up to order, holding hands.

I slide into the chair next to Josh. He gives my shoulder a squeeze, sending neurons zinging along my arm.

"I got you a medium Pure Peach." He smiles.

Strawberry Swirl. Pure Peach. Close enough. Josh's wearing one of his baggy ska band T-shirts. The blue letters—TUCSON TUNES—totally accentuate his Lake Havasu blue eyes. His shaggy light brown hair with chlorine-bleached streaks shines in the overhead mall lighting. And his megawatt smile lights me up inside like I'm a jack-o'-lantern.

"What took you guys so long?" he asks.

"Makeup kiosk. Did you see Junie's face? And

that's the new and improved version. How do I look?"

"Great, Sherry. Like always."

I glow. And it's not the face cream.

"Just don't stare at Junie. She's pretty sensitive about it all." I wasn't going to say anything, but I end up blurting out the whole story. "And everyone blames me. Which is totally unfair."

He gives my shoulder another squeeze.

Nick and Junie return with their juices. She chose a green tea mixture. Smart girl, remembering the skin revitalization diet.

"Sherry, with your science grade, I can't believe you experimented on Junie's and Brianna's faces." Nick pushes out a chair with his foot.

There he goes, giving me grief again. I force myself to get along because I don't want to mess up the double-dating thing, but I don't have to like him.

"No one knows exactly what went wrong, Nick," I say through gritted teeth. "Don't be so quick to pin it on me." Interesting that Junie confided in him. She's obviously tighter with Nick than I realized.

"You guys get any interviews lined up?" Junie forces a quick subject change.

"No, but we came up with a title. *Revealing Phoenix,*" Josh says.

I can tell by the way he juts out his chest that it

was his idea. Which doesn't surprise me. Josh is a well-rounded guy. He listens to music. He has loads of friends. He's a high-voltage water polo player. And he has the occasional scholastic moment.

"Our goal is to highlight a variety of slices of life in Phoenix. Josh is interested in interviewing security for the scoop on shoplifting, animals that wander into the mall, and the like." Nick slides the wrapper off his straw, then proceeds to fold it up, accordion-style. "I'd like to tackle more hard-hitting subjects— sales, finance, the economy."

Josh and Nick launch into a discussion of their many *Revealing Phoenix* ideas.

Yawn, yawn, yawn.

I scoot my chair closer to Josh's. Under the table, he reaches out and takes my hand. Now I don't care what Nick drones on about; I'm in hand-holding heaven.

From somewhere in the continent called my purse, my phone beeps out a text alert. I am so not letting go of Josh's hand to check my phone. So not.

"How about an interview with the information desk," Junie says. "They handle lottery ticket purchases—" She breaks off mid-sentence and pulls her phone from her jeans pocket. She frowns. "Sherry, it's from Amber. She needs to see us imme-diately at the kiosk."

I sip a little Pure Peach. I inhale a big whiff of

chlorine + laundry soap, l'eau de Josh. Our fingers are happily intertwined. And I hang there, content, immersed in this quiet moment of romance. "Uh, tell Amber I'm busy."

My phone beeps again. I ignore it again.

Junie's phone pings with a new text. "It's Amber." She slides her phone across the table to me.

<send sherry now! girl just returned naked makeup lip gloss cuz it burned her lips>

Ack. Eek. Ike.

chapter
five

Josh and Nick take off to do something video-ish.

Junie and I race over to Naked Makeup.

"Amber told me you're, like, a detective," Lacey says to me.

"'Cause of your mystery-solving experience," Amber says, "with the rhinos when we were in San Diego." She looks at Lacey. "Sherry even got her picture in the paper."

Puffy with pride, I feel like the Pillsbury Doughboy. "Junie was majorly involved too."

"Thanks, Sherry," Junie says.

"I need your help." Lacey's face is serious. "Desperately."

A mother in a wrinkled T-shirt and sweatpants

pushes a stroller with her sleeping baby. She rolls up to the kiosk.

Lacey sucks in a breath. I'm sure she doesn't want to spill in front of a customer.

"Hi, Courtney!" Amber says.

"I didn't realize you'd changed jobs." Courtney reaches into the diaper bag hanging from the back of the stroller and pulls out a blush container. "I was looking for you at the department store counter, and a girl sent me down here."

"Yay!" Amber says. "I'm glad you found me."

"Yeah, well, you're the only person who understands my skin tone." She hands the blush to Amber. "This is what you sold me at the other place. Got anything similar?"

"Similar, but better." Amber leans across the counter and starts flipping fast through containers of blush. "You will absolutely love Naked Makeup."

And she's right. Amber finds blush and eyeliner that Courtney can't resist.

When Amber's almost done ringing up the purchases, Courtney waves a package of pink emery boards. "Can you add this to my order? Or am I too late?"

With sparkling eyes, Amber looks up from the buttons on the register. "Courtney, you're chill."

Courtney's grin takes over her face.

Because when Amber beams on you, it's like she

43

invited you to the popular kids' lunch table. *And* is sharing her sandwich with you. This is why customers flock after her, following her from one end of the mall to the other, all to buy a bunch of makeup.

The second Courtney's out of hearing range, Lacey grabs my arm. "You have to help me, Sherry. This kiosk is the most important thing in my life."

"It's true," Amber says. "It's her dream career."

"I still work as a cashier at Discount Mart"—Lacey drops my arm—"but that's only till the kiosk brings in enough money to support me."

"Besides, Discount Mart's just a job." Amber draws out the *o* in "job."

"What happened with the lip gloss?" I ask.

Tongue between her teeth, Junie's überintent and paying attention. This is pretty much her style all day long at school. Which explains her nothing-but-As report card. The girl's professionally focused.

"Yesterday afternoon a girl bought lip gloss." Lacey taps her long decal-decorated nails on the counter. "She had it custom-blended."

"Watermelon," Amber says.

"And she returned it today." More nervous nail tapping. "Because it burned her lips."

"Any chance it's just a bad batch of gloss?" I ask.

If Lacey shakes her head much faster, it'll fly right off her neck and knock over a poor unsuspecting

44

shopper. "Naked Makeup is a good, solid all-natural product. I totally stand behind it."

Amber moves in close, so it's like the four of us are a clique. "It gets worse," she says.

Lacey shoves her hands in her lab coat pockets.

"Yesterday morning, for a different customer," Amber says quietly, "I mixed up a white-chocolate-plus-mint gloss. It was returned after I texted you about the first gloss return."

Shoulders stiff and tense, Lacey says, "Same complaint as the watermelon gloss." She opens a kiosk drawer and pulls out two absolutely adorable pink pots with butterflies on the lid. She hands them to me.

I open the pots and sniff. Watermelon and white chocolate + mint. I pass them to Junie.

She sniffs. "Did you try them?" She sets the pots on the kiosk counter.

"Yeah," Lacey says, "on our wrist."

I pick up the jar of Q-tips and hold it out to Junie like I'm offering appetizers.

"Only use a small amount." Amber gestures with her head to a few spritzer bottles by the register. "And don't move far from those. They're filled with water."

Junie and I each pry out a Q-tip. I dip one end into the watermelon pot and scrape up a smidgen of gloss. I flip to the other end and do the same for the white chocolate + mint.

45

I dab an iota of each on the inside of my left wrist. Junie watches me.

I hang.

Nothing.

Then a fizzy feeling prickles my wrist. Exactly the way Pop Rocks crackle and sizzle in your mouth.

"Yowzer!" It's as if someone pressed a lit match against my skin. I lunge for the spritzer bottle. And squirt. And squirt. And squirt.

Lacey grabs some paper towel from under the counter, folds it, drenches it with water from another spritzer and places it over my wrist. "This'll help."

"Imagine that on your lips," Amber says.

Ack. Eek. Ike.

Junie drops her Q-tip in the cute little pink trash can.

"What is it with Naked Makeup?" I press down on the paper towel. "First the night cream. Then the lip gloss. Beauty isn't supposed to be dangerous."

With short, jerky steps, Lacey paces the length of the kiosk. "It's not the makeup." She rubs her forehead. "Well, yes, obviously, it is the makeup." Now pacing and rubbing her head at the same time, she says, "The only explanation is that someone's adding bad stuff to the product." She stops all movement. "But why?"

"Do you have any enemies?" I ask. "Anyone mad at you?"

She shakes her head, her blond hair swaying back and forth like a curtain by an open window on a breezy day. "I've been racking my brain. No, I can't think of anyone who'd do this to me."

"Besides, I'm the person who sold all the sabotaged makeup." Amber points to her chest. "Could be someone's framing me."

"Who've you annoyed recently?" Junie asks her cousin.

Amber places a perfect nail on her perfect chin and makes a perfect indentation. "Beth Anderson. I'm dating her boyfriend. Sophia Hernandez. I did date her boyfriend a few times. Jonathan Mann, who I ditched after a few dates. My science teacher might have been insulted by the helpful acne-scar-reducing products I listed at the top of my quiz. Who else?" She stares off into the distance, blinking her heavily shadowed eyes. "My mom, my new stepdad."

It takes us less than a minute to come up with about ten people, mostly girls, who are peeved at Amber. But taking the investigation in this direction isn't clicking for me. Junie's furrowed brow says she's not buying Amber as the victim either.

"Amber, you definitely have more enemies than the rest of us put together," Junie says.

Amber stands straighter.

"But Naked Makeup isn't the most effective way to, uh, get to you," I say. "I think the target is Lacey."

47

Lacey sinks onto the barstool by the cash register. "Someone wants me out of business." Her head droops. "And if this mess keeps up, that's exactly where I'm gonna be."

Amber rubs Lacey's shoulder.

"When did you start using this batch of gloss?" Junie asks. "As in, do you expect more returns?"

Amber yanks open a drawer and checks some papers. "We opened the container three days ago. So, yeah, we could get more returns."

Lacey raises her head, grimacing. "And then there are the people who won't return the product but won't ever buy Naked Makeup again. Maybe they'll think they had an allergic reaction or that it's just lousy quality. All this is bad for business."

"Did you check the rest of the lip gloss base?" I ask.

Lacey kneels down and pulls a cardboard box toward her. From the box, she grabs a tub the size of a two-liter bottle of soda. She lugs it up to the counter.

I'm looking at the cardboard box. Specifically at the address label. "Do you always have your product sent to Discount Mart?"

"Yeah. Saves me from going to the post office to pick up packages." Lacey unscrews the cap and pokes in a Q-tip. "The Discount Mart guys keep it in shipping and receiving for me."

I clap my hands in sleuthing excitement. "Maybe

it's someone at Discount Mart." I so rock at this part of detective work. Where I come up with a million scenarios for what's possibly going on. "Like someone who works there is sick of babysitting your boxes."

Lacey frowns. "They'd just tell me to start shipping them to my apartment."

"Or maybe someone there can't stand you." I'm on a roll.

Amber slaps her hands on her hips. "Excuse me? *I'm* the one with the enemies, Sherry."

Not the only one.

"How about this?" Junie jumps in. "Maybe one of the employees doesn't believe in makeup, so they want your business to go under."

"Like the Janes," I say. "Do you have them at Discount Mart? This wacko group of girls who won't wear makeup 'cause they believe it sucks their attention away from their schoolwork and future potential."

"I never heard of a group like that at Discount Mart," Lacey says. "Word would get around pretty quickly, and no one would go on break with them."

"Or ask them out," Amber adds.

"Maybe Discount Mart is a red herring," Junie says.

Amber and Lacey look blank.

"A false lead," I explain.

"Anyway," Lacey says, "the packages are still taped

up when I get them. No one opens them. No one adds anything."

"Remember"—I cross my arms—"we're talking about the *shipping* department. Those people are expert tapers and sealer-uppers. They can break into your boxes, mess with the contents, then redo the packaging so it looks as good as new."

Lacey scrunches up her face in disbelief.

"Get a new idea, Sherry," Amber says.

I don't care what they say. I'm not discounting Discount Mart's shipping and receiving department yet.

"Lacey, try the base." Amber points to the Q-tip Lacey's still holding in midair.

Lacey dots a minuscule amount of the clear gel on her wrist. Within minutes, her eyes are watering and she's blinking up a storm. "Definitely contaminated." She squirts water on the affected area with a spritzer bottle.

Amber pins me with her emerald (thanks to colored contact lenses) eyes. "So, Sherry, what's in the gloss?"

Palms up, I say, "Beats me. I have a C in science."

"Time for an acid test," Junie says.

chapter
six

Junie and I hoof it over to my house. According to my brainiac BFF, we need sodium bicarbonate to test for a chemical reaction. Sodium bicarbonate is a fancy-schmancy name for baking soda.

We could build a small cabin with the number of boxes of baking soda The Ruler keeps in our pantry. Or bake a loaf of bread the size of Arizona. Or place a bowlful of powder in every fridge in the nation.

Why so much baking soda? Because The Ruler washes all our fresh fruits and vegetables in a water + baking soda mixture. To get rid of pesky leftover pesticides. Which there shouldn't be any of because she buys organic. There's no reasoning with her in this area.

When Junie and I arrive, The Ruler's in the kitchen, whipping up a couple dozen cranberry–orange juice muffins. They're überyummy, but deceptively disguised as überyucky with their lumps and sickly color.

The Ruler is misleading in the same way. At school, with her stiff posture, strict rules and severe tests, you'd never realize that she's actually Ms. Maternal. At this very moment, wooden spoon in hand and flour in her hair, she's mixing batter in our kitchen.

"Junie, your face is looking much better." The Ruler pours a cup of orange juice into a large ceramic bowl. "And yours is almost completely cleared up, Sherry."

"They did our makeup at the kiosk. Plus, they gave us special cream," Junie says. "And I have a spray too."

While The Ruler cracks brown eggs and sifts wheat flour, we fill her in on the makeup scandal.

"That's terrible. And it could be very dangerous, depending on the contaminant." She dumps a cup of cranberries into the bowl and gently folds them into the batter. "You know, the Nut 'n' Nut carries all-natural makeup."

Buy my makeup at the health food store? Who wants to be beige and boring and smell like basil? Not. Me. Not. Ever.

"Sounds like a safe alternative," Junie says.

The Ruler smiles wide.

This is why parents love Junie; she always says the right thing.

"Actually, Naked Makeup'll be super safe again soon. Junie and I are going to figure out who's behind the sabotage."

"Do you really think someone's purposely tainting the makeup?" The Ruler bends over to pull out the baking pans. "It's probably full of toxic chemicals. Just because the name 'Naked Makeup' sounds natural doesn't mean it is."

"It's botanical," I tell her. "And styling." I grab a couple of glasses and the apple juice from the fridge. "Lacey believes someone's out to ruin her business."

The Ruler plops batter into the muffin pan, nodding in that absentminded way adults nod when they don't buy into what you're saying. Which is fine. If she actually knew the risks I've taken when solving mysteries, she'd triple-lock me in my room.

I grab a cereal bowl from the cupboard and a box of baking soda from the pantry. "We brought the messed-up lip gloss, and we're gonna mix it with baking soda."

That sets The Ruler and Junie off on a science chat where they're bonding over pH balance and hydrogen molecules and acids versus bases.

After a few sentences, I interrupt. "Why exactly are we doing this?"

Junie's stirring up a paste of baking soda + water

in the bowl. "Trying to figure out if an acid was added to the lip gloss."

"But, basically, we're watching for bubbles?" I wanna keep this simple.

"Exactly. Lots of bubbles"—Junie pops off the gloss pots' lids—"means the mystery ingredient is super acidic."

The Ruler stops filling the muffin pan.

The three of us stare into the bowl.

Junie spoons in some watermelon gloss. Nothing happens.

Junie spoons in some white chocolate + mint gloss. Still nothing happens.

"So"—Junie carries the bowl to the sink—"the mysterious ingredient isn't an acid."

"Well, what is it?" I ask.

"Beats me." Junie turns on the faucet.

The Ruler doesn't say anything, but her toxic-commercial-cosmetics expression speaks volumes. She opens the oven door and slides in the muffin pan, then twists the timer knob.

"Sherry, when the timer goes off, remember to pull out the muffins." The Ruler heads to our office to catch up on her grading.

"Okeydokey artichokie." Ack. Did I really say that? My dad's rubbing off on me, in a bad-joke kind of way.

I text over to the kiosk to let them know what Junie and I discovered. As in, no acid in the lip gloss. Amber and Lacey text back that they checked the rest of the makeup and it was clean. Yay!

"Well, at least Lacey didn't have to throw out any more makeup," I say. "Other than the lip gloss."

"Yeah, that saves her some cash," Junie says.

I nod and we sink into the couch in the living room.

"You going to ask your mom to help with the makeup mystery?" Junie asks.

No one living is supposed to know about the Academy of Spirits, but one day, when I had a big meltdown, I spilled to Junie.

"I'll summon her tonight."

My pesky, perky eight-year-old brother, Sam, explodes into the room, interrupting our conversation. "Sherry, Dad and I got some sick supplies for my business!"

"What business?" Junie can afford to be über-interested because she's an only child and doesn't have the tiresome task of dealing with a little brother 24-7.

"Selling organic plants and vegetables from our garden. Including a bunch of cacti. Paula and I grew them." Sam's Tigger-bouncing all around the room. "You should see the wagon I just got. And a change box."

55

"What will you do with all the money you make?" Junie asks.

"I'm not saying." Sam grins from sticky-out ear to sticky-out ear. My brother and his secrets. He should grow up and join the FBI.

Sam's a much happier kid since I managed to wangle five minutes of Real Time for him with our mother. He and Mom spent five minutes at Dairy Queen, face to face, where he could talk to her, see her, touch her. As per Academy rules, he doesn't remember the experience, but he's back to being the annoying brother he was before Mom's death.

"A timer's buzzing," my dad calls from the kitchen.

Junie and I bomb down the hall. I grab the oven mitts and pull out the muffins.

Junie sniffs big. "These are the yummiest."

"Hi, Junie. Always good to see you." My dad walks over and tweezers out a muffin with his index finger and thumb. "Ouch." He drops it on the counter and blows on his fingers. "And, of course, always good to see you, pumpkin."

I swear I will never call my child a vegetable name. I will probably stick to gemstones.

"Sam, come help me unload your stuff from the car!" Dad shouts.

Watching the two of them walk out to the garage, I can't help but notice how they're like mis-sized twins with an identical dorkity-dork bouncing walk.

Junie checks her phone. "I gotta go home."

I slip a couple of muffins in a Ziploc bag for her.

She gives me a quick hug and whispers in my ear, "Good luck tonight."

chapter
seven

It's late and dark and spooky on Saturday night. My flashlight flickers. Probably it needs new batteries. Damp, clammy grass licks the soles of my feet as I creep through the backyard to the ornamental pear tree. My mom planted this tree when I was born, and it's where I always have the best luck getting her to show up. She's only flying from across town—the Academy is located in Dairy Queen—but it's a big challenge with her horrible sense of direction.

I swing a leg over the lowest limb and drag myself up. I get positioned and comfy . . . well, as comfy as you can get on a bumpy branch in the middle of the night. My back smushed against the trunk, I wave an open bag of Costa Rican espresso coffee beans and think Mom thoughts. Then I wait.

Thud! The tree shakes. I dig in my heels to keep my balance.

"Hi, Sherry." The branch dips as my mother settles beside me. "Ooof. Rough landing."

I inhale. My mother was überaddicted to coffee when alive, and a mild java scent follows her wherever she goes now. Nutzoid and weirdo as it sounds, I can smell ghosts. And their smell is always somehow related to their mortal time.

Mom quizzes me about school and Sam. She even asks after my fish.

We chill for a little in silence, that comfortable kind of silence between two people who know each other well. My girlfriends spend time with their moms in the kitchen or the car or while shopping for clothes. For me and my mom, it's a little—well, a lot— different. But I'm just happy I get to be with her at all.

"So, Mom, something weird's happening at the mall." And I launch into the whole Lacey + Amber + tainted makeup story.

When I'm done, she says, "I wonder what the abrasive ingredient is. And is it the same for the night cream and the gloss?" I bet she's twirling her hair around her index finger, mulling it all over. It's a mother-daughter habit. "You and Junie only tested the gloss for acidity, right?"

"Yeah, because Lacey already sent the cream to her head office for analysis." I hug my knees. "But The Ruler—Paula said there was a small amount of papaya acid in it.

"You sound positive the factory isn't just sending bad batches."

"Yeah, I am."

"You've certainly had enough detective experience that you can trust your gut."

A bubble of pride zings around inside me. "Thanks."

"You want to help this girl out?"

I think of Lacey grabbing my arm and how desperate she is to save her dream business. "Definitely." I hook my hair behind my ears. "But it's more than that, Mom. It's personal for us. You should see Junie's face. Brianna and I are mild. It's not okay to do that to people and get away with it."

There's a wispy light breeze as my mom touches my face. "Your skin's still dry and red. Why don't you stop wearing makeup for a while?"

"What?" I practically roll off the branch at the absurd suggestion. "Go out in public without makeup? Seriously? And have you forgotten I have a boyfriend?"

My mother sighs. "How's that going?"

"Fantabulous. We're actually going on a movie date tomorrow."

"Your father and Paula are okay with it?"

"Basically." It's my turn to sigh. "But I have to come straight home after the movie. And it's a *matinée* on a *Sunday*."

"You have to wear makeup on this, uh, date?" Mom stumbles over the word "date."

I stretch out my legs and cross my arms. "Yes."

Silence. Not as comfortable as before.

"I'm surprised the Phantom Security Squad hasn't brought up any of the incidents," Mom says. "It's not like them to miss offenses committed against humans. I attended the most recent Academy security meeting, and the PSS didn't mention a cosmetics case."

"They're only human—oops." Because they aren't human. Just like my mom, they're ghosts with a background in law enforcement or detective work.

"Perhaps the goings-on at Lacey's kiosk are such small potatoes that the Academy's not getting involved," Mom muses.

The bubble of pride grows into a bubble of excitement. "Well, then this would be a perfect opportunity for us to earn Real Time. We discovered our own mystery. We solve it. We keep loads of humans safe from tainted makeup. The Academy is überproud of us. And, voilà, they award us five minutes of Real Time." Then the bubble of excitement kicks it into high gear. "Do they ever award more than five minutes of Real Time? Like, how about a day. Think of how great it would be to spend an entire day together! Where I could actually see you."

There's a long pause. Too long.

"I can't help with the makeup situation," Mom says slowly. "And I don't think you should either."

chapter
eight

It's Sunday morning around eleven. Lugging a heavy backpack, I hopped a bus and now I'm standing in front of Dairy Queen. Make that Dairy Queen, aka the Academy of Spirits.

I so don't want to go in. But I gotta find out why my mom can't help me on the cosmetics case. And change that. Sigh. A detective's got to do what a detective's got to do.

I square my shoulders, pull open the heavy glass door and step inside.

Yikes.

A million and one rug rats in Little League uniforms are bombing around, screaming and screeching. What are their parents thinking? Play a baseball game and we'll reward you with humongous amounts of frozen empty calories?

Yikes. I mentally slap myself upside the head. Why am I going all judgmental about junk food? The Ruler and her food views are rubbing off on me. Ack.

"Excuse me, excuse me." I fight my way to the back of the store and the secret entrance to the Academy. Oh great, six more kids, even louder than the ones I squeezed by, are sitting, jumping, hopping at the back table with their coach.

I've never tried to pass through the secret door with witnesses. It's probably not allowed. It's probably more painful than usual. It's probably impossible.

I hang a left into the restroom. I unzip my backpack and tip it over. Out spills my bike helmet, my large owlish sunglasses and a roll of heavy-duty aluminum foil. Crossing the threshold to the Academy is no mean feat. If not done properly, it hurts. As in a trillion electric shocks snapping and zapping at me. My hair'll stand on end. I'll see stars. My legs'll go numb.

I dress for the mission.

Bike helmet on: Check.

Large, owlish sunglasses on: Check.

Tinfoil wrapped around arms and legs: Check.

I push open the door.

Six bratty kids eating sundaes the size of their heads point at me.

"Coach! Coach! Who's that?"

"Coach! Coach! Is that a homeless person?"

"Coach! Coach! Should we call the cops?"

"Hi, kids!" I say, all fake cheerful and party-voiced.

"Howdy, Coach!" I raise an arm in a crinkly wave. "I'm the new mascot for Dairy Queen. Captain Silverpants."

"I gotta pee," says the smallest team member.

The coach grabs his hand and bounds into the restroom.

Which leaves me with ten staring eyeballs. Unfriendly eyeballs. And one of them's bloodshot with pinkeye.

"You're a Dairy Queen mascot?" A short, squat boy squints at me. "How come I've never seen you in a TV commercial?"

"Uh, Captain Silverpants is a brand-new mascot." I paste on a sugary smile.

"Why're you wearing a bike helmet instead of an ice cream cone?" says a tall, runny-nosed boy. "And your costume is cheap. Like you made it in your kitchen. Without adult supervision."

"Maybe we're inventing a new ice cream treat?" I say. When did this generation get so jaded?

"Aren't you Sam's sister?"

Captain Silverpants is striking out. I'll never get past these hoodlums and into the Academy.

"You're a fake!" says the boy with pinkeye. He winds up his leg and kicks me in the right shin!

"Ow!" I can't believe it. These are the worst-behaved, meanest kids on the planet. And they're guarding the secret door to the Academy. I bend over to rub my poor aching leg, and discover his nasty pointy cleats ripped small jagged holes in the aluminum foil!

"Fake! Fake! Fake!" yells Pinkeye, who proceeds to plant his cleats in my left shin.

"Ow!" I'm hopping up and down, dodging metal-cleated kicks from Pinkeye, when a couple of the other monsters start pulling at my aluminum foil. "Get away from me, you brats!"

The short, squat boy leaps at me from a bench seat. He knocks my helmet crooked.

Then, *flash!* A brilliant home run of an idea slams into my mascotish mind. "Look! Free double-chocolate-dipped cones at the cash register!"

The gang beelines to the front of the store.

I shove open the Employees Only door and slide across the threshold. Thousands of electric arrows zap and ping, ping and zap. "Ouch! Ouch! Ouch!"

My bike helmet askew, I fall to the floor moaning. Electric shocks pierced the torn aluminum foil. My legs tremble. My head aches. My eyelids droop. I mumble in pain.

Yes, I made it to the Academy. But I'm half dead.

chapter
nine

I lie curled up on the linoleum floor of the Academy. There's got to be an easier way.

The smell of Cinnabon breezes past me. My mother's guidance counselor, the powerful and moody Mrs. Howard, is arriving.

"Howdy, Miss Sherry." A blurry snowballish shape hovers above the only table in the room.

I can see a fuzzy Mrs. Howard when she allows it.

An arm extends from the shape and points to a small Oreo Cookies Blizzard. The Blizzard slides obediently to the end of the table nearest me.

I lurch to the table and collapse on the bench. Grasping the cup, I sip and sip and sip. Finally, I gasp, "Tough entrance."

"Sure enough, you are a survivor, Miss Sherry. We've witnessed this several times," Mrs. Howard drawls. She's a Southern ghost with an accent that can lull you to sleep. She can also morph from a welcoming Cinnabon smell to a burnt-sugar odor faster than a bobcat can climb a tree.

"I might need another Blizzard," I pant. "I usually order a medium."

"To what do I owe the honor of this unexpected visit?" Mrs. Howard floats above me.

I tell her about the tainted makeup and finish with, "I really need my mom on the case with me."

"Have y'all discussed this?"

Slurping, I nod.

"And what exactly did your mama say?"

"She didn't think she could help, but she wouldn't tell me why. So, I climbed on a bus, faced injury and humiliation from a horde of Little Leaguers, and traveled through the Portal of Pain into the Academy just to talk to you." I clasp my hands together and beg. "Could you please assign my mother to the case?" Even though Real Time hovers at the edge of my mind, I do not even dare mention it. One favor is already pushing the limit with this bossy, controlling ghost counselor.

A rectangular plasma screen appears in the upper corner of the room. "Honey, go on and watch this."

I crane my already cricked-out neck.

Shimmering and glowing, the screen fills with headlines.

Mother-Daughter Duo Pulls It Off

Mother-Daughter Teams: Wave of the
Academy Future?

Living Teen Masters the Silver Box

A Mom, a Girl, a Wren, a Rhino

A black arrow cursor blinks its way across the screen and double-clicks on MOTHER-DAUGHTER DUO PULLS IT OFF.

Who is this ghost mother and living daughter who teamed up to solve mysteries for the Arizona Academy of Spirits?
Meet Christine Baldwin, former detective with the Phoenix Police Department. Christine is an entry-level ghost with a background in K9.
Meet Ms. Baldwin's daughter, Sherlock "Sherry" Holmes Baldwin. Sherry is a thirteen-year-old student at Saguaro Middle School in Phoenix, AZ. Sherry talks with her mother but cannot see her.
Last March, the two joined forces to fight evil in San Diego, CA.

The scrolling speeds up, so I can only catch a word here and there: "successful," "courageous," "quick-thinking."

"What *is* this?" I ask.

"The WWWD," Mrs. Howard says. "The World Wide Web for the Dead."

My jaw drops. I am speechless.

"And, as you can plainly see, you're plastered all over it. There's even a YouTube video of you investigating the rhino enclosure at the Wild Animal Park in San Diego."

My jaw is still gaping. I am still speechless.

"You and your mother are receiving a bushel-load of attention. 'Hits' I believe it's called." Mrs. Howard balloons herself up big and bloated. "Which can be good." A burnt-sugar smell seeps into the room. "And which can be bad."

Placing the back of my hand under my jaw, I manually close my mouth.

"Academies all over the world have their specter eyes upon y'all. Our allies are rooting for us and applauding our creativity in putting you and your mother together to crack cases. Our enemies, however, are waiting in the wings for you to fall flat on y'all's faces, bringing shame and ridicule upon our entire organization."

"I've always wanted to be famous," I blurt out.

"Now listen carefully, missy, 'cause this is fixin' to

get real complicated. There is a foreign Academy we've been attempting to form an alliance with for years. Each time we approach them, they turn us down. Suddenly, they're interested. Why? Because they want to hire your mama. She's our in: They hire her, we hire one of their agents."

I slide my sunglasses down my nose and gaze over them Hollywood-style. I would so rock at famous.

"But the deal isn't sealed. Not even close."

I plop my helmet on the table, then twist my hair into an updo. Fame will never go to my head. No, no, I will remain my normal friendly self, except with a boa and air-kissing. I'll chat and chatter with my fans, signing autographs with a fat, glittery pen.

"Our potential alliance must remain secret."

Leaning back, I cross one leg over the other and, toes pointed down, swing the top leg à la movie star. I. Am. Famous.

"Sherry, have you listened to a word? Do you know what in the Sam Hill I've been talking about?" Mrs. Howard's right in my face, so close I could put my hand right through her. If I so desired. Which I do not.

I swivel my head, posing and smiling for an imaginary camera. I parrot back, "The Academy is über-anxious to hook up with a powerful foreign Academy. The foreign Academy wants my mother. We want an agent from them. It's all confidential." The last word barely escapes my lips when my brain overrides my fame fantasies and kicks into high gear. I jump up. My sunglasses clatter to the floor. "Who's the foreign Academy? What's Mom's talent? How long would they keep her?"

Mrs. Howard shakes her oversized doughy head. "There's too much at stake."

"I can keep a secret."

Silence. An embarrassing silence. While we both think of how I spilled my guts about the Academy and my mother to Junie. And how maybe keeping secrets isn't my thing.

Mrs. Howard breaks the silence. "If the PSS has not brought this makeup mys-ter-y"—she pronounces "mystery" slowly, not treating it seriously—"to our attention, it's not worthy of our talents."

Like an annoying yappy dog, I spring up and down. "Look at this." Still jumping, I point with both hands at my cheeks. "You can't tell me this is nothing." *Up. Point. Point. Down.* "This is something." *Up. Point. Point. Down.* "This is worthy of your talents."

I sink onto the bench, panting.

"Sherry, you're a teen. Y'all have skin problems."

I'm too exhausted and out of breath to argue.

Growing and expanding like an inflatable holiday snowman, Mrs. Howard floats up and stretches across the ceiling. The room is thick with an over-cooked syrupy smell. "There is no cosmetics case at

72

the Phoenix Mall; it is merely a cosmetics inconvenience. This inconvenience will not be handled by our Academy. Not by your mother. Not by you."

Mrs. Howard's voice grows louder and bounces off the walls.

"In fact, the higher-ups in our Academy have decided to not give you or your mother any work. Your mother must devote all her energies to passing the difficult tests in the foreign Academy's strenuous ongoing interview process. It is imperative for us that our two Academies finally join forces.

"Your job is to lie low. Maintain a code of circumspect behavior. Do not encourage further exposure on the WWWD. The foreign Academy is watching you. Your actions reflect on your mother and on us. Don't give the foreign Academy any reason to reject your mother's application."

Yikeserama.

A medium Oreo Cookies Blizzard floats through the wall and slides across the table to me.

"Thank you kindly for visiting, Miss Sherry. Your services are not required at this particular moment in time. Return to your own world, where you can be a normal teen"—Mrs. Howard pauses—"who behaves herself."

Poof! She's gone. Along with her overpowering, sickly sweet cinnamon-bun smell.

I ignore the Blizzard. I stand, stick my sunglasses

on my nose, straighten the aluminum foil around my arms and legs, and strap on my helmet.

In fearless-explorer style, I toss my backpack over my shoulder, take a deep breath and march to the door.

During the brief moment when I have one foot in the Academy and one foot in Dairy Queen, when half my body is under attack by sharp blue zapping pings, I make a decision.

A decision Mrs. Howard won't like.

chapter
ten

I ride the bus to the mall, where I vainly attempt to repair my looks in the restroom. Without a ceramic iron to tame my wild and woolly hair. Without the incredible skin-repairing china clay. After ten minutes of hard work in front of a cloudy mirror, let's just say *Seventeen* magazine won't be calling me for a photo shoot. Unless it's a "before" shot.

Junie and I planned to meet at the food court before doing some investigative work. But I text her to come to the restroom instead.

"I don't know if I should be out in public, asking questions," I say the second she arrives. "I look like I'm practicing for Crazy Hair Day at school while boycotting sunscreen."

Junie rolls her eyes. "Your hair looks fine. Maybe a little fuller than usual. And don't even talk to me about skin. At least your face doesn't look like it fell on sandpaper. Besides, we already agreed to split fries."

I'd forgotten about the fries. While we're walking to the food court, I give her the short version of my visit to the Academy.

"Let me get this straight," Junie says. "You go to the Academy to ask for your mom's help with the case. You leave the Academy and your mom can't help, you're supposed to drop the case, *and* foreign ghosts will be spying on your behavior."

"Basically." At the American Potato Company counter, I ask for a large fries.

"Are you going to follow Mrs. Howard's orders? And drop the case?"

"No way. I can't do that to Lacey. I can't do that to us."

"You know you can count on me." We bump knuckles.

"Here's what I'm thinking," I say. "If the PSS is ignoring what's going on with Naked Makeup—"

"It must be a simple mystery." Junie sprinkles salt on our fries. "Which means—"

"We can solve it," I say, loving this BFF-finish-the-sentence thing. "Easy—"

"Schmeasy. And Mrs. Howard will be begging you

to take five minutes of Real Time with your mom as a reward."

"And I'll be even more famous on the WWWD, and the foreign Academy—"

Junie shoves the cardboard boat of fries at me and sticks her fingers in her ears. "Do not tell me any secrets. Seriously. I do not want to know what I'm not supposed to know."

I chew furiously on a fry. When I get excited, my mouth takes on a life of its own, flapping and spewing away. And now I can't remember exactly what was secret and what wasn't. What I'm allowed to share and what I'm not allowed to share. Which means I have to keep all of it to myself. Wah!

Junie unplugs her ears. "Is it safe?"

"Yeah. I'm under control." I squirt ketchup in the corner of the boat. "Something Mrs. Howard never brought up? My grandfather."

My grandfather's fiercely loyal and has a great sense of direction. He'll be a good help with this mystery.

Junie grabs a fry. "So, it's you, me and your grandfather." She dunks the fry in the puddle of ketchup. "Plus, Nick and Josh can help us."

"Let's get going!"

Junie pops the fry in her mouth. We both push our hair behind our ears so that our cute matching best-friend earrings dangle and swing. Then, legs in sync, we stride off for some important mall recon.

"The plan is to check out the entire mall and see what other stores and kiosks sell makeup, right?" Junie's got a determined look on her bleached freckled face. The same look she gets when a teacher's passing out a big test.

We wander past every store on every level.

At the entrance to the department store, we stop. We can see the makeup counter where Amber used to work till she quit for Naked Makeup. Amber's ex-boss, Crystal, is packing nail polish into a box.

"What do you think?" I say. "I mean, Lacey and Crystal are competitors, but they're such good friends. Amber says the three of them eat lunch together and share beauty tips."

"Right after she switched jobs, I asked Amber how weird it was to still be at the same mall. She told me to grow up, that I just don't get the makeup world." Junie shifts her fake leather purse on her shoulder. "Maybe if we were a couple of years older and had part-time jobs in the cosmetics industry, it wouldn't seem weird. Maybe we're just too thirteen."

And that, in a nutshell, is why I love having Junie on my team. She's beyond smart.

At the Beauty Connection, we pop in to check out the merchandise.

Junie opens and sniffs a bottle of foaming bath oil. "There's some overlap between the stuff in here and

78

Naked Makeup's inventory, but Lacey's products are much higher-end."

"Not to mention no one works here for more than a week." Which is handy for Junie and me. We come in to use their free samples almost every weekend, and no one recognizes us or asks us if we're ever planning to buy.

I hold up a black-with-white-polka-dots cosmetics bag that would fit perfectly in the front pouch of my backpack. "Cute?"

"Go for it," Junie says.

Mall recon and light shopping go hand in hand. In the bookstore, Junie buys a magnetic bookmark with the periodic table. At Brittani's Baubles, I find a striped lipstick holder with a miniature mirror inside. Which I definitely need. I remember to get my card stamped. Only four purchases to go before I'm eligible for my freebie. Although I see several more items of interest, I hold back. I gotta save a little money to buy snacks at the movies later with Josh. He's covering the cost of the tickets, and I'm in charge of popcorn and candy and drinks.

If my dad could see me and my careful shopping habits today, he'd be forced to eat his "Sherry spends her allowance like we've got a money tree in the backyard" words. And, honestly? I'd be way more financially responsible if I had more money. I so need a major raise.

In terms of cosmetics competitors likely to sabotage Naked Makeup, Junie and I are coming up with zilch. There are several stores that sell some makeup, but not one that specializes in it.

Finally, we're on the last section of stores. We discuss skipping it because our feet are übertired. Also, this part of the mall is like the desert at the edge of town. As in, it's deserted. But Brianna told me there's often free tortilla chip samples, and my stomach's grumbling from all the walking. The french fries were miles ago.

We pass the under-construction vitamin store, the out-of-business shoe store and a closed-on-Sundays fabric store.

Then, suddenly, a chili pepper is dancing toward us. It's the hot-sauce kiosk guy decked out in an embarrassing puffy red outfit with tights and an ugly green cap for a pepper stem. Even more embarrassing, he has no rhythm.

Still high-stepping, he waves us over with skinny stick arms. "Free samples. Free samples."

Ya don't have to say that three times.

Junie and I head for the hot-sauce kiosk, which, actually, is attractively decorated. Mini chili-pepper lights blink around the forest green awning-roof. Different-sized and-shaped jars of various kinds and colors of salsa and hot sauce and whole chilies line the shelves, along with aprons, T-shirts, caps and even jigsaw puzzles. There's a pyramid of prickly pear cactus jam. And a stack of prickly pear cactus candy. Bags of fresh peppers hang from hooks. Who knew Phoenix was home to an entire subculture of chili pepper lovers?

Best of all, a large ceramic bowl of free tortilla chips and three small matching bowls of complimentary sauce sit on the counter.

"What are the sauces?" Junie asks.

The kiosk guy ends his jig. His face all sweaty, he points a skeletal finger. "Mild, medium, deadly. The deadly is extreme heat. It's five hundred times hotter than a jalapeño pepper." He picks up a small, thin bottle and shakes it. "Snake Spit. With habanero pods." He hands the bottle to Junie. "Don't even think about trying this undiluted." .

Junie reads the ingredients, then plucks a chip from the basket and scoops up some mild sauce.

Personally, I'm going straight for the deadly. I've never tried it before, but I was practically born eating Mexican food. When my mom was alive, our favorite family restaurant was Tio Roberto's. And there was nothing on the menu too hot for me. Habanero pods will be a walk in the park.

I dip a chip and pop it past my lips and directly onto my tongue. Definitely spicier than usual. But flavorful.

I dip another chip. I turn to ask Junie about the

mild sauce. I miss my mouth. The chip + deadly sauce collides with my lips.

For, like, two seconds, there's a fizzy, tingly feeling on my lips. Then it's like someone's holding a lit match up against them.

"Yowzer!" I fan my mouth with my hands. "Hot, hot, hot!" I'm fanning fast, at airplane propeller speed. "Water, water, water!"

Junie grabs my arm and drags me to a water fountain. Which means warm, murky water with unidentifiable floaties. But I'm desperate.

I twist the knob with a jerk and submerge my lips in the arc of brackish water cascading from the faucet.

Finally, the pain subsides enough that I can gasp out, "My lips are burning. Like with the lip gloss!"

chapter
eleven

Huffing and puffing, Junie and I arrive at Lacey's kiosk. When the chili pepper guy wasn't looking, I grabbed the bowl of deadly sauce.

Miraculously, there's a lull in business at Naked Makeup, and we can actually talk to Amber and Lacey. Good thing—I'm not sure I could have prevented my mouth from blurting out our discovery. Even in front of customers.

"Snake Spit burned my lips like the tainted lip gloss!" I plunk the bowl of sauce on the kiosk counter.

Amber and Lacey, who are both cleaning with pink feather dusters and rearranging bottles and jars, turn at the same moment. Two beautiful, but confused, faces.

"Speak English, Sherry," Amber says. She is not known for her manners.

"You know the kiosk over by the out-of-business shoe store? The hot-sauce place with the weirdo vendor? Anyway, I dipped a chip in this bowl of habanero sauce." I'm talking all breathy and at roadrunner speed. "At first, my lips went tingly, which wasn't too bad, but then they were painfully, crazily on fire."

Lacey and Amber are still looking beautiful and vacant.

"Like the contaminated Naked Makeup lip gloss!" Junie says. "We think the mystery ingredient is the same ingredient that's in the super hot sauce Snake Spit."

"Another lip gloss was returned." Lacey opens a drawer, pulls out a little pot of gloss, then twists the cap off. With a Q-tip she paints a little gloss on her wrist, then pokes the other end in the sauce bowl. She drips it on the same wrist.

After a minute or so, she grabs a water spray bottle. Pressing the trigger faster and faster, she washes down her arm. "Felt exactly the same."

"But the sauce is red." Amber does not offer a wrist. "None of the returned glosses were red."

" 'Cause the sauce has tomatoes," Junie says. "But

if you squeezed the juice from the pepper, it'd be clear. The active ingredient is capsicum."

"He sells peppers too," I say.

"I know the guy you're talking about," Lacey says. "Will. He seems pretty nice. I can't see him contaminating lip gloss."

"If by 'nice,' you mean 'loser,'" Amber says. "And someone needs to tell him to eat another helping at dinner. Pencil thin is not attractive." Amber always judges people by their looks. "And he's such a whiner." She opens a drawer and drops in her duster, then gets to work tightening lids on bottles of hand lotion. "Always complaining he never has any customers and how it's not fair we're so busy. What does he expect with a kiosk off in the back forty?"

My heart speeds up. Because this is what we detectives call motivation. "How do you get assigned a kiosk location?"

Lacey shrugs. "First come, first served. I guess I happened to put my application in before him."

"What happens if people keep on having reactions to Naked Makeup?" I ask. "And you get a bunch of bad publicity? And customers go to the mall manager and complain?"

"I'm sure the mall'd kick me out," Lacey says. "The manager's a major control freak." She gnaws on the tip of the long nail of her index finger. "So, you're thinking Will tampers with my product and gets me in trouble with management? Then I get the boot, and he moves to my well-located kiosk?"

Junie and I are nodding like a couple of bobble-heads on a sugar high.

"I can see it," Amber says. "Will is wacko weird."

"Of course, there's the problem of how he's getting the habanero juice in the lip gloss," I say.

"And we don't know what made us break out from Nite Sprite Creme." Junie touches her cheek.

"We don't even know that Wacko Will's up next if your kiosk comes open," I say. "Could be some other business would move in."

"Hi, girls!"

We all jump like we're in a horror movie and a big hairy tarantula lunged at us. We were so intent on sauces and glosses and kiosks that we didn't even hear Crystal approach.

"Girlfriend!" Amber squeals. They hug. "How are you?"

"Busy." Crystal smiles at Amber.

Lacey and Amber and Crystal dive into a big gripe session about the janitors at the mall and how they're all slackers with no apparent schedule for trash pickup, because they just come by whenever they feel like it. Junie and I are totally shut out from this inner circle, which gives me a chance to stare uninterrupted at Crystal.

Where Amber and Lacey have shoulder-length blond hair and porcelain skin, Crystal has short black boy hair and the hugest chocolate brown eyes. She's seriously married to bling and wears tons of it, from hoop earrings to several silver necklaces of different lengths to arm bracelets to ankle bracelets to toe rings. She's very metallic and glittery.

The three of them, with their gorgeous hair and nails and makeup, stand chatting and complaining and laughing. It's hard not to sigh at the sight of such beauty.

"Guess what I scored, girls?" Crystal fans herself with a bunch of coupons. "For the new pretzel place." She passes a handful to Lacey. "They are so yummy."

She turns her gaze on me and it's like being in the white warmth of a spotlight. "That is the cutest denim purse I've ever seen. I am so digging the silver studs."

"Thanks," I say. So on top of her great looks and generosity with coupons, she has incredible taste in purses.

Crystal pushes a circle of bracelets up her slender arm. They tinkle down, glittering. "Lacey, what can you tell me about Eve?"

"Eve?" Lacey says. "Who used to work for me?"

"Yeah," Crystal says. "She filled out an app to work for me."

"Reliable, polite," Lacey says. "But she couldn't

work the hours I needed. For a very part-time employee, I think Eve'd be good."

"She wasn't so polite when Lacey let her go." Amber's lining up miniature bottles and filling them with white cream. "She stomped the whole way out the door."

Junie pokes me in the side. I know exactly what that poke means: A disgruntled, stomping ex-employee makes a fine suspect.

"She's coming in for an interview tomorrow after school." Crystal runs her fingers through her hair. "Lacey, Amber, did a man come by? Somebody's husband. Gray hair, basketball stomach, Discount Mart jeans? He was returning lip gloss his wife bought yesterday."

Amber waves the container of gloss Lacey just tested on her wrist. "Yeah, we refunded him."

"He tried to return it at my counter," Crystal says. "I guess his wife had an allergic reaction? Anyway, I recognized the gloss and sent him your way."

"Doesn't look like it was an allergic reaction." Amber goes back to filling the little bottles, all the while explaining about the other lip gloss returns and the habanero sauce and my slumber party fiasco with Nite Sprite Creme.

Crystal gazes first at my face, then at Junie's. She touches Junie's cheek. "It does look like a chemical burn."

The whole time Amber and Crystal are talking, Lacey's head is down. She's fake-tidying-up the counter, just moving items back and forth. Her hands are shaking.

"Have you ever had a bad batch of makeup, Crystal?" Lacey asks in a small voice.

"I haven't." Crystal's frowning. "Did you contact Naked Makeup about it, Lacey?"

"I did. They haven't had any complaints from other vendors," Lacey says. "Not even vendors with product with the same lot numbers. I sent in Nite Sprite Creme samples to corporate for testing."

"Will you send in the lip gloss too?" Crystal runs the bracelets up and down her arms.

"I could." Lacey presses her palms flat on the counter. They stop trembling. "But if it's the hot-sauce ingredient . . ." Lacey trails off.

"Capsicum," Junie inserts.

"Yeah, capsicum," Lacey says. "Corporate wouldn't test for that."

"We're convinced someone's sabotaging Lacey." Amber's screwing lids on the mini bottles. "To, like, put her out of business. We don't know for sure, but Sherry thinks maybe someone's adding capsicum to our lip gloss. She's done some detective work in the past and she's trying to figure it all out."

Junie's eyes flash.

I try to add that Junie's working on the case with

me, but Amber barrels over me. She never worries about Junie's feelings. Probably because they're cousins—she knows Junie's stuck with her.

"If I were you, I wouldn't keep sending tainted makeup to your headquarters," Crystal says. "They'll start getting very anxious about what you're selling and question whether they should shut you down to keep their name clean."

Crystal leans in, looking closely at Junie again. "Cross your fingers that it ends soon and you don't have any more incidents." She straightens. "I'll keep my ears open and let you know if I hear anything."

"Thanks," Lacey says, all choked up.

"We're gonna keep working hard, hooking people up with Naked Makeup because we totally believe in the product line." Amber's unrolling lavender ribbon and cutting it into lengths of about six inches. "We're gonna find out who's doing this to Lacey and stop them. It's our duty as cosmeticians."

Lacey hugs Amber.

"What're you working on?" Crystal picks up a strip of ribbon.

Amber points to the miniature bottles. "Silky Soft Hand Lotion. Hands love it. It's the perfect product for introducing shoppers to Naked Makeup." Amber is positively glowing. She believes in this product from her highlighted head all the way down to the tips of her painted toenails.

"We're decorating samples to give away." Lacey's hands are steady now as she picks up a bottle.

"Junie and I can help after school! We'll walk around the mall with a basket, handing them out," I say. "We'll reach more customers than if the samples are just sitting here at the kiosk."

Amber and Lacey squeal at the same time.

Junie nods, which goes to show how far she's advanced socially. Not too long ago, she would've chosen math homework over giving away free samples of lotion.

"I gotta boogie," Crystal says. "I left Suze in charge and you know what a pain she is if I'm gone too long."

"Seriously," Amber says.

Suze isn't part of the Amber-Crystal-Lacey trio.

"Thanks for the coupons," Lacey says. "And for the moral support."

"No prob." Crystal waves and her bracelets tinkle and sparkle.

Amber's gazing at me like this is science class and I'm a bug under a microscope. "We'll do your makeup before we send you out to represent Naked Makeup." She turns her scientific gaze to Junie. "You can help Sherry in a few days. Your face needs to heal."

Junie flushes red like a tomato. Which makes her face look even less desirable for advertising Naked Makeup.

"I'm sorry, Junie," Lacey says.

"Can I wear a lab coat?" I ask. Professional makeup people always wear lab coats.

"Sure," Lacey says.

Junie looks like she wants to hit me.

"I'll pull your hair back too," Amber says. "So you look older."

I totally feel like my fairy godmother sprinkled growing-up dust on me. With Amber working on me, I'll leap all the way to seventeen.

Only one thing can make life better than this. And that's time with Josh.

The countdown is on for our movie date!

chapter
twelve

Josh Morton and I have been a romantic item for the serious amount of time of two months, three weeks and five days. I can't tabulate the number of hours or minutes or seconds, because it's difficult to pinpoint exactly when a relationship begins.

Despite the length of our time together, I still get flutters whenever I see him. Even if we're only waving to each other across the courtyard between classes. At the moment, it's like a fly swatter's in my stomach flapping up a storm. Because we're actually going on a date. Our first movie date ever. It's a defining life moment, like learning to ride a bike or getting braces or passing your driving test.

Mostly Josh and I hang together at my house or at

his or we grab something from Jazzed-Up Juice at the mall. We generally don't even eat lunch together at school because we only have the same lunch period on assembly days.

I'm pacing in front of the movie theater, waiting for Josh and getting more and more annoyed with Junie. Why did she have to start an argument with me. Now thoughts of her are barging into my brain and, like her, they're too stubborn to leave.

Things with Junie were humming along, all fine and friendly, until I mentioned my movie date. She jumped in with how she and Nick would love to come along. I hesitated. Which she noticed because she can be very observant in that way. She asked difficult, pointed questions, such as why didn't I like Nick and why wouldn't I give him a real chance?

In vain, I tried to explain the concept of a first movie date and how it isn't an appropriate double date. I described the whining and crying and turned-in homework necessary to wring a yes from The Ruler and my dad. How I've been waiting for years for my first movie date. How I just don't want to share.

Junie couldn't get it through her 4.0 skull. Now that I'm mulling it over, probably she hasn't had a boyfriend long enough to understand. Anyway, she ended up calling me selfish. And I may have said a couple of unkind things about Nick.

Pace. Pace. Pace.

If only I could concentrate on Josh. Josh with his pool-bleached scruffy hair. Josh with his chlorine + laundry soap scent. Josh with his baggy T-shirts and sagging jeans.

Pace. Pace. Pace.

But no, there's Junie buzzing into my mind again. She's like an irritating redheaded fly.

The more I pace, the more nervous I get. I mean, what do I know about movie-date protocol? Do I sit on Josh's right or left? Do we share a drink? Do we try to hold hands with a soda towering between us?

Then there's the whole kissing question. Will he? What if the people behind us complain? But will he? What if the people behind us know The Ruler or my dad? And what does it mean if he doesn't?

Junie. Josh. Soda. Kissing. It's enough stress to ruin a perfectly good date. I shut my eyes and take deep breaths. Where's The Ruler's calming chamomile tea when I need it?

"Ah!" I scream. Someone pinched my waist.

Whirling around, I open my eyes.

"Sorry, Sherry. I didn't mean to scare you." Josh smiles. The patch of freckles dotting his nose looks particularly adorable today. "Well, uh, I did mean to scare you, but not that much."

"Junie's really mad at me because I didn't want to double-date this afternoon." The words explode out of my mouth like horses from the gate at the start of a race. Who knows what I'll say next? *Are you planning to kiss me during the movie?* I clamp my lips firmly shut. My mouth can't be trusted under pressure.

Josh doesn't even blink. "That wouldn't have worked. Nick's meeting a friend of his dad's who has ideas for our *Revealing Phoenix* video."

Yay. Who knew that annoying video project would ever come in handy?

"You could text her about next weekend," he suggests. "How about miniature golf?"

I pull out my phone, tap in a message and punch Send.

"Wanna buy some candy from the drugstore before we go in?" Josh asks.

Brilliant idea. Because movie theater candy costs a mint. That's from my dad, King of Bad Puns and Jokes. I keep it to myself.

Junie replies back that next weekend works for putt-putt. It's not the friendliest text, but friendly enough that I let the my-BFF-is-mad-at-me worry disappear into the stale mall air.

Josh takes my hand and we set off. "So, what movie do ya wanna see?"

"Definitely not horror."

"Okay." He proceeds to give me the lowdown on each of the movies. Very impressive. He did his date homework. At each new detail, his blue eyes twinkle with excitement. Especially when he talks about the movie *Renegade Racers*.

It's impossible to not have fun when we're together. A movie date is turning out to be as amazing as I always imagined. And the movie hasn't even started.

In the drugstore, we get our candy and a bottle of water to share. I easy schmeasy fit all the loot in my humongous, beautiful denim purse. I toss it over my shoulder and practically knock myself into the shampoo aisle.

While we're walking back to the theater, swinging arms like a cute couple, I bring Josh up to speed on the mystery. I so love talking detective together.

"You really think this Will guy's dumping habanero juice in lip gloss?" Josh asks.

"A lot of times, crime is about opportunity. How easy it is to get your hands on something," I say. "And it's super easy for him to get hold of habanero chilies."

With his free hand, Josh snaps his fingers. "What if Nick and I interview Will for *Revealing Phoenix*? We'll try to get him to admit something sketchy on tape."

That's Josh, my enthusiastic yet cool boyfriend. A very tough combo to pull off. "Great idea!"

He grins across his entire dreamy face, showing off his perfect white teeth and his little dimples.

We get decent seats in a middle row with no tall people anywhere in the near vicinity. I forget to worry about whether to sit on the left or the right of Josh.

The lights dim. The previews start. Then *Renegade Racers* kicks off. I have a Tootsie Pop in one hand and Josh's hand in the other. I'm totally owning this movie-date thing.

Until the moment I smell coffee.

My mother!

chapter
thirteen

"**W**oo-hoo! Sherry!" my mother calls.

Ack. Eek. Ike.

My mother is somewhere in the theater! Hunting me down. Why oh why did I tell her about my movie date!

With her zero sense of direction, I can't believe she even found her way in here. Hopefully, she can find her way out. I scrunch low in my seat.

If I'm quiet and all incognito, she'll move on to the cinema next door. There are eighteen theaters in the complex; that should keep her busy for hours.

I scrunch down a little further.

Josh gives my hand a boyfriendly squeeze. "Don't

worry, Sherry. It's way too early in the movie for something major to go wrong."

I nod. Weakly.

"Sherry!" Mom calls. "Are you in here?"

"Oh, wait. This part might be gory," Josh whispers. "Maybe you should cover your eyes."

Which, of course, makes me stare straight at the screen.

A guy lunges from behind a trash can, wielding the longest, meanest knife in the history of bad guys. I understand he's leaping for the good guy. I really do. But he looks like he's leaping out of the screen. Right at me.

I scream.

"Oh, there you are, pumpkin." The scent of coffee is right beside me. Right between me and Josh. Sort of hovering over where we're holding hands.

I scream again.

Josh is looking at me like maybe I need to take a chill pill. "You wanna go out in the hall for a minute?" he whispers. "It's going to get scarier than this."

"Yeah, yeah, I'm outta here. Woo." I drag the back of my hand across my forehead like I'm wiping off fear sweat. "This is such an edge-of-your-seat movie."

"Uh, sure," Josh says.

"I'll see you in the hall," Mom says.

I stand.

Josh stands. He's such a nice guy.

But no, I don't need a nice guy right now. I need a word with my mother the ghost. A strong word. By myself.

"You make a better door than a window," a guy behind us says.

"I'm good. I just need to, uh"—I pat my chest—"catch my breath."

"Anytime soon," the guy says.

I put a hand on Josh's shoulder. "Seriously. You stay."

He sits.

"Finally," the guy says.

I hightail it outta there. Like I'm in a real-life chase scene.

The second I enter the lobby, my mom's flying next to me. "Hi, pumpkin. How's it going?"

I walk into the photo booth in the corner, holding the curtain open until I figure Mom's had enough time to zip in.

"What are you doing here?" I sit down on the narrow plastic bench. "You came to spy on me, didn't you? Admit it, Mom."

"Well, no, not exactly."

"Really?" I cross my arms. "When was the last time you went to the movies?"

"Don't think of it as spying, Sherry. Think of it more as chaperoning."

"Mom!" I wail. "You're ruining my movie date."

"That's just it. I think you're too young to be going on a real date. I'm okay if you and Josh rent a movie and watch it at the house. This is different. This is older teen behavior."

"The thing is, Mom," I say softly, "I can't have three parents. Especially if one of them is The Ruler, who, all by herself, is like a parent and a half. You and I, we're just getting our relationship figured out."

"Oh." Her voice is choked up.

"What you did is unfair and unethical." I uncross my arms. "Just because you're invisible and you *can* sneak in and spy on me doesn't mean you *should*." I raise my shoulders. "You gotta trust me. You gotta trust that I'm okay going to a bad movie with a good guy."

"He really is a good guy?" she asks in a small voice.

"The best," I say. "And even if he wasn't, the movie date won't be happening again for a long, long time. You do not even want to know the hoops I jumped through to get here."

"You're so mature." Mom lifts my bangs with a light, feathery touch. "When did my little girl do all this growing up?"

"I've been growing up for a while now. I think you're forgetting that I'm thirteen." I pull open the curtain.

"Sherry, while I'm here, I do think there's something we need to discuss."

"Fine." I close the curtain but keep some fabric bunched in my hand.

"I got called in to see Mrs. Howard," Mom says. "About your visit."

"Oh."

"I just want to make sure you understand how much is at stake."

"Okay."

"It's difficult to talk about because it's so on the q.t., and there's so much I can't say." She sucks in a breath. "Our Academy is dealing with some domestic issues that have their roots on foreign soil. So, it would be really, really helpful if we had a relationship that allowed for information and personnel sharing with this foreign Academy."

It's all vague-ish and political-ish, but I'm getting the gist. "Mom, I won't mess up." Just the opposite. I'll be wowing everyone by solving the makeup mystery.

"And about my opportunity with the foreign Academy?"

I let go of the curtain. This isn't going to be the shortest chat.

"It will just be temporary. I won't leave you and Sam. I don't want you worrying about that. But, oh, it's the chance of a lifetime." She catches her breath in excitement. "Here's what I can tell you. It's working with animals, exotic animals. It's a huge challenge, but I'm up for it." She pauses. "And, Sherry? I'm doing stuff with animal mind control that nobody else in the world is capable of doing. It's incredible."

"That's fantastic. I'm proud of you, Mom." And I really am. My mother's come a long way from the ghost who couldn't master her classes. The ghost with such low grades, she was on the verge of getting kicked out of the Academy. The ghost who took months learning to fly across Phoenix.

"I'm glad we had this chat, Sherry." The curtain slides open. "Now, go back to the movie. And have fun."

chapter
fourteen

The so-called movie date is over. I'm hanging out in my room, having a heart-to-heart with my bala sharks before hitting the pillow. It's been a tiring weekend.

I sprinkle a little fish food into the tank. Cindy and Prince immediately zig and zag, dodging each other and the mini fake castle. With their tiny mouths flapping open, they're gobbling as much of the fish flakes as they can.

"Cindy and Prince, you guys do not know how lucky you are. You get to swim and frolic together in the same tank all day long. While *I* have to make big, complicated plans in order to spend time with the love of my life. Sometimes all goes smoothly. Sometimes it's the Rocky Mountains."

Sitting cross-legged on the carpet, I stare into the aquarium. "So, guys, let me tell you the story of a movie date gone bad. Start with a lousy show called *Renegade Racers,* which, as far as I could tell, was very short on plot and very long on chase scenes and bad guys wielding pointy knives. Then add in an overprotective ghost mother who actually shows up during the date. On purpose. And spends so much time chatting with me in the hall that Josh thinks I'm a scaredy-cat wimp with a stomach bug who was in the restroom for the bulk of the movie. Finally, I come straight home and do way too much homework. I do not think Josh and I will be going on a movie date again anytime soon. Which is A-OK with me."

I hop up and set the lid back on the aquarium. Bala sharks are stupidly willing to leap to their deaths. And I so don't want a carpety fate like that for my precious pets.

Falling back on my bed, I wave to the ceiling. "Goodbye, today. And good riddance."

Tomorrow just has to be better.

chapter
fifteen

My alarm clock chimes its obnoxious wake-up-and-get-out-of-bed-for-school chime. Monday mornings can be so unwanted.

I slowly unfold myself and sit up. I yawn. My head aches and my eyes are scritchy-scratchy. I did not sleep well, but dreamed all night long of bad skin and upset friends. My crazy new age grandma, who is big into dream interpretation, would say my subconscious is trying to warn me.

Not that I believe in any of that hocus-pocus, but, just in case, I'm keeping an eye out for potential problems.

I glance across the room. Cindy and Prince are

swimming around the aquarium. No sad belly-up floating scene. Phew.

My white tank top, black-and-blue-plaid baby-doll and black cropped pants hang happily behind my door. No rips or wrinkles or stains. Phew.

I listen at the door of the bathroom I share with Sam. I'm up before him and can take my sweet time in the shower and then in front of the mirror. Phew.

I make it through my morning routine. Even my skin has way improved, and I camouflage the remaining redness with a thickish layer of foundation. I pay particular attention to my azure eye shadow and navy mascara.

Junie texts to say she's staying home from school for an additional day of face healing, but that she's not counting on me to pick up homework assignments for her. She already contacted Meghan, her responsible, academically minded friend from the robotics club. Junie still plans to catch up with Eve after her interview with Crystal later today.

I'm out the door, backpack over my shoulder, skipping to school. No complications. No catastrophes. No calamities.

I start a happy whistle. The dreams were just that—dreams.

I'm trundling along the sidewalk in front of the school, minding my own business, totally lost in my own world. I'm trying to figure out where I might cross paths with Josh today. By the giant stone saguaro cactus statue in the courtyard between Computer and English? Then I'm trying to remember if I finished all my homework. Then I'm wondering exactly when that pesky *français* project is due.

Bump! A hip knocks into me from the right.

Thwack! A backpack bounces off me from the left.

Whop! A binder flattens against my spine.

Jostled and shoved, I finally catch my breath and my balance and look around.

I'm surrounded by a group of the plainest, sullenest, unhappiest girls at Saguaro Middle School.

The Janes. Ack!

I glance around the circle of pale, lifeless faces. I'd be scared but it's broad daylight. In fact, the sun beams down on their makeupless faces, accentuating every bump, every blemish, every blackhead. Also, I know them from classes. Although now it's kind of hard to tell them apart because they all look bland and milky. They blend together like a crowd scene in a black-and-white movie.

I catch sight of a friendly face. "Brianna!" I reach toward her like I'm drowning.

Brianna lifts her head and looks straight at me.

I can honestly say I've never seen her looking worse. Even compared to last year when she had the stomach flu and had to go to the hospital because she was dehydrated. Today, evidence of the Nite Sprite Creme fiasco still shows on her face in pink scaly patches. *Foundation alert.* Her eyes are small and squinty and unaccented. *Mascara and eye shadow alert.* Her cheeks are sunken. *Blush alert.*

"Brianna! I've got makeup." I pat my backpack. "I'll fix you up. Just pull me out of this circle of drab and we'll hit the restroom before first period."

"Brianna's giving up makeup," Jane #1 says. Actually, her name is Emily, but I prefer to number the Janes.

"Yeah, right." With my index finger, I make the universal circular sign for crazy by my ear and point at Jane #1.

"It's true," says Jane #2, aka Tess. "Brianna wants a fulfilling career."

"So?" I say.

"I joined the Janes." Brianna's normally perky, high-pitched voice is all monotone.

"And we want you to join us too," says Jane #3, aka Kim.

"Thanks, but no thanks." I step back. "I'm pretty happy the way I am."

"Middle-school girls who are not obsessed with makeup get better grades. Which leads to better colleges. Which leads to fulfilling professional careers." Jane #1 closes the gap between us. I think she might be their leader. She's certainly the palest.

"Kim already told me." I shrug. "I wanna work in

beauty. I need to know a bunch about makeup for that. So, when you think about it, I'm getting a jump start on my career by wearing makeup in middle school."

"I told you she'd be impossible," Kim says, exasperated.

"I am so not impossible." I slap my hands on my hips. The Janes are one annoying school club. "Am I trying to win you over to my side? Am I forcing you to wear makeup? No. You want to look lackluster and fade into walls painted neutral colors? That's your choice."

The Janes shuffle closer and closer, hemming me in. They're fluttering wet wipes in my direction.

"Try a day with us," Jane #1 says. "We can have you makeup-free in seconds."

Now I'm a little nervous. These girls are not normal. It's like they ate bad meat or something, and it turned them pushy and rabid. I'm waiting for them to start drooling.

Sweat beads on my upper lip. I straighten my shoulders and plaster on my tough, confident face. You have to look in control with bullyish people. Or, apparently, they'll wipe off all your beautifully applied makeup.

The first bell rings.

"There's a direct link between being on time for class in middle school and college scholarships," I say.

The hands stop waving their wet wipes.

"Let me save you from yourself," Jane #2 says.

Whatever, strange girl. I have no idea what she's blathering on about.

Speedy like a roadrunner, she unzips my backpack and snatches my brand-new polka-dot makeup bag. I stocked it this morning with the idea of carrying it back and forth to school so that I'm always prepared for between-class freshen-ups.

My arm shoots out to seize it, but she spins and is gone. She's fast for an ugly girl.

"Hey, Jane! Stealing's against school rules. I'll report you."

The rest of the Janes scurry off like cockroaches. Brianna's swept along in the middle of them.

Kim's at the back of the pack, herding the Janes down the sidewalk.

Kim, who came to my slumber party.

Kim, who refused a makeover.

Kim, who had ample opportunity to mess with the night cream.

That's a lot of Kim.

chapter
sixteen

One class left to go and then I'm jetting to the mall to pass out Naked Makeup lotion!

I trudge into French. Madame Blanchard is at the front of the room, back to us, scribbling nonsense on the whiteboard. Her bottom wiggles and jiggles like aloe vera gel.

Dealing with Madame Blanchard is like calling someone's cell only to be sent to voice mail. Over and over. As in, you never get through. Überly frustrating.

For example, what is the deal with not letting us choose our own partners for projects? Why stick me with Kim? Do French people not understand the concept of friends?

And what about geography? Madame Blanchard forces us to speak French, and only French, *la seconde* we step into the classroom. I have pointed out, in vain, that this is Saguaro Middle School, where the official language is English. I can't get through to her, though, because I'm trying to say it in French.

And now I have to explain—in French—why I can no longer work with Kim as my partner. This morning, the Janes drew a line as wide as the Grand Canyon across the sidewalk, and I'm on one side while they're on the other. There is no meeting in the middle for foreign-language projects.

I take a deep Frenchish breath and approach the polyester mass by the whiteboard. "*Bonjour,* Madame Blanchard." I paste on an international smile.

"*Bonjour,* Sherry."

I figure French women invented makeup, which explains why so many of them (obviously not Madame Blanchard) personify beauty and sophistication. So, probably makeup terms are all French words. "Kim *est* Jane."

"*Pardon?*" Madame frowns.

How can she not get a simple sentence like "Kim is Jane"? This is exactly why we should not be speaking French in French class.

I start over and say with exaggerated lip movements, "Kim *est* Jane. Kim *est grosse.* Yuck. Yuck." I make a grossed-out face. "*Non, non,* Kim *n'a pas de* mascara." I mime brushing on mascara and waggle my finger to show *none*. "*Non, non,* Kim *n'a pas de* lipstick." I mime swiping on lipstick and waggle my finger again. "*Non, non, Kim n'a pas de* blush." I mime patting on blush while shaking my head. "*Oui, oui,* Kim *est* Jane."

Madame Blanchard regards me, hands on wide hips and thick penciled-in eyebrows raised.

I jab my chest with my thumb. "Sherry *est* Sherry. Kim *est* Jane. *Non projet.*" I lift my arms, crossing, then uncrossing them to show, without a shadow of a doubt, that Sherry and Kim do not mix.

Smiling, I step back. I've done an excellent job of getting my point across. In French.

A flush of anger begins at Madame Blanchard's double chin, then spreads over her doughy face. She blasts forth a long string of sounds, heavy in the vowel department, which I can only assume is French at freeway speed. Her voice gets louder and louder. Finally, with a sausage finger, she indicates my desk and turns her back on me.

I did not understand one single word of her tirade, but still the message came through loud and clear. I'm stuck with Kim. There is no democracy in France. Madame Blanchard hates me.

I slump into my seat.

"Thanks a lot," Kim mutters under her breath. "She docked us an entire grade because you insulted her."

"What? How?" I sputter. "I wasn't insulting her. I was insulting you."

"You called her fat."

"What? How?" I sputter some more.

"*Grosse* means 'fat' for a woman in French. And Madame Blanchard's first name is Kim."

"How do you know her first name?"

"She told us."

I bet she told us in French. Ooh la la. I bury my head in my hands.

I think time in France moves slower than it does in our country. And these same minutes crawl along, unhurried and annoying, in French classes around the world too.

But, finally, the last accent mark is drawn, the last verb is conjugated and the last page of homework is assigned.

I power outta there, off school property and over to the mall. I cannot wait to be transformed by Amber. I cannot wait to cruise the mall, bestowing Naked Makeup samples on lucky shoppers. I cannot wait to be seventeen. If only for a couple of hours.

The minute I arrive at the kiosk, Amber's down to business. "Have a seat and I'll do your face and hair." She sticks my backpack in a drawer. "Leave that here so you don't look so middle school."

That Amber, she thinks of everything.

I end up giving her my huge purse too. No point lugging it and the lotion samples around.

I perch on the little stool by the cash register. "Where's Lacey?"

"Working at Discount Mart. Her shift's over in about an hour." Amber tugs my hair back into a ponytail. "We want you over by the main entrance, off Van Buren, with the basket of samples." She's like a juggling act with brushes and creams and powder. She's talking at me, not to me, concentrating on my forehead. "That's the busiest entrance. I got a bunch of bottles ready." She gestures with her elbow, not skipping a beat at patting cream into my cheeks. "They turned out cute, dontcha think?"

I turn to look and she grabs my chin like it's a handle and pulls my face back to her. A couple more swipes with a sponge and she swivels my head. "See?"

Miniature white plastic bottles lie nestled on butterfly fabric that spills over the edges of a wicker basket. Wrapped around each bottle is either a lavender or pink ribbon with curled ends. And each bottle has a tiny label: *Silky Soft Hand Lotion by Naked Makeup.*

My heart soars. I love those little bottles. I can't wait to hand them out. It's my first mall job. Minus the paycheck. "They are adorable, Amber."

"Of course they are." Amber presses powder on my

nose. "And, before you ask, I checked the samples yesterday afternoon. No problems." She chooses a small brush and a couple of shades of green shadow. "Close your eyes." She dusts my eyelids.

I figure with each stroke of her brush, Amber's adding a month to my age. I'm probably up to fifteen years old by now!

"Open your eyes. Look up. Don't blink." She sweeps on mascara. "You know how to act, right? Polite. Professional. Stand straight. Smile. No chatting with your little friends. Only approach women. Yes, some men do buy lotion, even makeup. But most of our clients are women and we have a limited number of samples." Amber is all adult and business-ish. I've never heard her talk so fast. "Make sure they know where the kiosk is. And that the products are botanical."

Amber's one of those people with a knock-you-over personality. When I'm with her I always feel like I'm at the bowling alley. I'm a pin and she's a fourteen-pound ball.

With her thumb, she smudges something at the outside corners of my eyes. "And don't do your giggly thing."

"What giggly thing?"

She rolls her eyes, her eyelashes practically grazing her forehead. "Look, Sherry, we're counting on you. This morning Lacey had another returned gloss. The woman said she was going to blab to everyone at her office about it. We need some good publicity today. And that's where you come in."

My stomach knots up at the pressure.

She undoes the ponytail and fluffs my hair. "Perfect." She hands me a mirror. "You're done."

Wow. I look amazing. Seriously amazing. And at least seventeen. Maybe even seventeen and a half. "Wow. Thanks."

She just nods and tosses me a lab coat. She's too cool to say you're welcome. "Your skin's looking good. Junie'll take longer." Amber's scooping up all the tools and storing them in a drawer. Very organized.

I gently glide my arm through a sleeve of the lab coat, pull it on, then slide in my other arm. Instantly, I feel older and more mature and professional. It's like magic.

Amber hands me the basket. "Remember, we're counting on you."

I was recently a bridesmaid in my dad and The Ruler's wedding, and I've still got the whole gliding wedding walk down pat. So I'm coasting along, my wedge sandals barely tapping the shiny linoleum floor.

I'm trying my best to look professional, but it's impossible not to slouch because the basket is way heavy, like it's filled with bricks, not cute little Silky Soft Hand Lotion samples. The handle's seriously chafing my arm, most likely cutting off important blood supply. I hug the basket closer to my body, where it bangs awkwardly against my left hip. Not helpful. Now I'm walking bowlegged with locked knees. I'm like a cross between a penguin and Little Red Riding Hood. This is certainly not the look Amber was aiming for.

Far off in the distance, like an oasis, I spot the main entrance doors. Who knew our mall was the size of a mini city? Traveling from Naked Makeup to the front entrance is an Olympic workout. I'm actually sweating and my back, arm and leg muscles are tightening up.

I pick up the pace. If I can just get near the entrance and a nice comfy bench. Surely, giving out the samples from a seated position will be professional enough. My neck has a crick. My arm is numb.

I decide to sprint the last mile. Breathing heavily, bent over like a pretzel, I focus on the bench. Bathed in sunlight, it's my pot of gold at the end of the rainbow.

Wedge heels are not worn by runners for a good reason. Wedge heels are to ankles like scorpions are to crickets. Deadly.

My feet race down the wedges and right off the sandals. My left foot turns back to look for its footwear while my right foot continues on in the marathon. My right side has always been a little more competitive. Which explains why I'm right-handed.

My poor left ankle is all turned in and weak. I fall heavily. The basket thuds to the floor, toppling over. Many adorable bottles of Silky Soft Hand Lotion are released into freedom, rolling every which way. Their purple and pink curlicue ribbons twist like little piglet tails.

I lie on the floor, grasping my ankle and groaning. Hopefully in a professional manner. I am definitely not doing my giggly thing.

A circle of concerned shoppers forms around me. A mother turns the basket right side up. She instructs her children to chase down the rolling bottles and return them to the basket. A mall security guy peers down at me. "I have nine-one-one on speed dial."

"Sherry, are you okay?" Junie offers me her arm. She's like a guardian angel who shows up right when I need her.

I pull myself to a wobbly stand. "I don't need nine-one-one." Leaning on my BFF and balancing on my uninjured foot, I say, "Junie, could you pick up the basket?" I look around at everyone. "I'm fine. Seriously. Thanks for grabbing all the bottles, kids."

I pick out bottles from the basket. "Samples, anyone? Free Silky Soft Hand Lotion, a botanical product from Naked Makeup." I point a shaky finger. "The kiosk is by the food court."

I am so not following instructions. I'm offering samples that have rolled all over the mall floor and were retrieved by the sticky fingers of small children. I'm giving away lotion to anyone who gets close to the basket—men, women, kids. And the way I'm hanging on to Junie isn't even close to professional.

People start reaching into the basket and plucking out bottles all on their own.

A girl about my age with purple streaks and huge dangly earrings says, "What scent is it?"

I stop. I never thought to ask. "Good question."

Junie already has a bottle open and up to her nose. "Jasmine, I think."

I stick my palm up by her. She tips the bottle and white lotion cascades out. A light flowery scent fills the air.

I rub my hands together.

"Ahhhhh!"

chapter
seventeen

Ack! Eek! Ike!

Something's in the Silky Soft Hand Lotion!

Something not silky. Something not soft. Something very thin, prickly and pointy. Many of these somethings.

We're back at the kiosk. Amber and Lacey are examining my hands. A deep wrinkle of worry creases Lacey's forehead.

"How many of the bottles did you get back?" Lacey asks me.

"About five," I say.

"How many did you give out?" she asks.

"Ten? Maybe twelve? I don't know." I'm in such

pain I'm having trouble staying with the conversation. "It's hard to know how many rolled away."

Lacey's eyebrows jump up to her beautiful blond hairline.

"Think, Sherry," Amber snaps.

"Well, basically my feet were racing in opposite directions—"

Junie jumps in and explains how she was coming through the doors and saw me fall and the lotions go skittering all over the floor. I'm sounding decidedly unprofessional in this story. "Even thought she hit the floor hard," Junie says, "she still worked at giving out samples."

With a paper towel, Amber scrubs at my hand.

"Ouch! Ouch!" I say. "What're ya using? Sandpaper?"

"Sherry, don't be such a baby," she says. "I'm just cleaning the lotion off."

I close my eyes and grit my teeth in the hopes this will reduce the hot poking pain. Not working. When she stops scouring, I crack an eye. Yikes.

Amber's holding tweezers like she's going into battle. And my poor tortured hand is the enemy. "Close your eyes," she orders, then proceeds to attack my palm.

I jerk away. "Ow!"

She waves the tweezers and smiles. "Got one."

I seize the tweezers and stare at a light-colored,

needle-sharp sliver. Up close, I can see that my hands are filled with them. They're under my skin, poking through my skin, some shallow, some deeper. "Junie!" I wail.

She brings my hands up to her glasses and really scrutinizes. "They're from a cactus. I think."

I swing my hip toward her. "Call The Ruler. Speed-dial two. She's a gardening expert."

Junie pulls my cell from my pocket, presses two, then holds the phone up to my ear.

"Help! Spiny things are stuck in my hands. Help! Help!" I'm hysterical. And itchy. Itchy like I was stung by a billion mosquitoes.

Junie grabs my phone and speaks with The Ruler. When she clicks off, she says, "Glochids. They're very fine bristles found on cacti like the prickly pear. Apparently, there are some prickly pears by the south doors of the mall."

I'm flapping my hands in the air.

"She said you need white glue," Junie says. "Squirt it all over your hands, let it harden, then peel it off. That'll pull out the glochids."

"White glue? No hospital visit? No painful shots?" I feel better already.

"She said you'll be fine." Junie slips the phone back in my pocket. "But she's worried because you were freaking out."

"I'll call her back after we do the glue."

"Sherry, let me get this straight." Lacey squints an eye, concentrating. "You stopped giving out samples the second this happened?"

I nod.

"You asked for the samples back from the customers still standing around?" She's counting bottles, grouping them in little families of five.

I nod.

"We're short three bottles." Her arms fall to her sides. "Three bottles. They could be on the floor where you fell, right?"

I gulp. "I guess."

"Or with shoppers," Amber says.

"Hopefully, on the floor." Lacey looks like she's going to cry. "If we don't locate the missing bottles in half an hour, I'll have the mall make an announcement."

"I'll help you look," Junie says.

"I'm going to the drugstore to pick up glue," I say. "Then I'll meet you guys."

Amber stretches out an arm, "The lab coat, Sherry?"

I rip it off, glad to be back in my own comfortable clothes.

Amber stays behind to man the kiosk, check the bottles of lotion to see if they all contain glochids and check the rest of the product.

I limp to the drugstore, my hands tingling.

Lacey and Junie take off at a run.

chapter
eighteen

After leaving the drugstore, I stagger to a bench, pull the red cap off the glue with my teeth and saturate my left palm. The glue is actually somewhat soothing.

Yes, people are looking at me like maybe they should call security. But there comes a point with pain where you just don't care what society's saying.

I stumble to the main entrance. The shopping bag's slung over my right arm, while I hold my left hand up like it's balancing an imaginary tray.

Junie and Lacey are coming toward me.

"Guess what?" Junie calls out.

"What? What'd you guys find?"

"All the bottles are accounted for." Lacey's swinging

her arms and smiling. She's carrying two bottles of lotion. Junie's got the third.

"Guess what else?" Junie says. "These three bottles don't even have glochids in them. So not all the lotions are contaminated. That's gotta mean something."

I'm still holding out my left arm, gluey palm facing the ceiling. I shake my poor stinging right hand. "Yeah, like maybe someone was shoving in the prickles and got interrupted."

"We checked out the prickly pear cacti." Lacey takes the third bottle from Junie. "The bristles on them look exactly like the pokey things in your hand. It's impossible to tell if yours came from those same cacti, because the plants are covered in the things."

"But, still," I say, "the habanero juice in the gloss *could've* come from Wacko Will's kiosk. The bristles in the lotion *could've* come from the mall garden. So, both those items are potentially local."

"Maybe the ingredient in the night cream is from close by too," Junie says. "And we just don't know yet."

We're back at the kiosk, waiting for Amber to finish up with a customer before continuing our conversation.

Lacey plunks the three lotion bottles on the counter.

Amber makes a fist in the air. "You found them all.

I checked the rest of the lotion samples. Five more bottles were filled with those pointy things."

Lacey's face falls.

"But," Amber continues, "I went through all the opened product in the kiosk. Nothing."

"Amber, what time were you done making up the samples?" I ask.

"Yesterday afternoon," she says.

"So the glochids were added between yesterday afternoon and today after school," Junie says. "Who was working at the kiosk then?"

"We both were, sometimes together, sometimes alone." Lacey's voice falters. "I'm really grateful for all the help, guys, but I'm totally creeped out that someone hates me enough to be doing this." And the wrinkle crosses her forehead again.

"Depending on the suspect"—Junie squeezes Lacey's arm—"it might not be personal at all. More about money."

The glue's dry and cracking on my palm. Junie pulls it off. Miracle of miracles, the slivers really do peel right off with it. And without pain. All that remains is a little tingle. The Ruler knows her gardening.

"Was there anyone strange around the kiosk between yesterday afternoon and when I arrived today?" I squirt glue over my long-suffering right palm.

Amber bounces the tips of her fake nails off each

other, thinking. "I can't remember anyone strange, can you, Lacey?"

Lacey shakes her head. "It was busy, so there were lots of customers."

"Any shockingly plain customers? Like the Janes?" I ask.

"We often sell to girls who are buying makeup for the first time," Amber says. "So it's not unusual to have people hanging around with no makeup on."

I describe Kim, with her perfect oval face. "She's a Jane who was at my slumber party and refused to use the Nite Sprite Creme. Maybe because she'd secretly doctored it up when the rest of us weren't paying attention. Or maybe a bunch of Janes were here and distracted you guys while one of them messed with the cream."

Lacey's as white as the glue on my hand.

"How about Will?" Junie asks.

"Will's always here," Lacey says. "He eats at the food court every day."

"It's not just Will either," Amber says. "Lots of mall employees stop by to say hi or buy something when they're on break or at lunch. Almost everyone hits the food court at some point during the day."

"Well, it seems to me that we have five possible suspects so far." I hold up a white finger. "Wacko Will, who might be next in line for your kiosk." I hold up two white fingers. "Kim or even a gang of Janes with their ridiculous hatred for makeup." I wiggle three white fingers. "Someone we haven't even thought of yet." And then I raise four fingers. "Eve, an ex-employee who left in a bad frame of mind." I wiggle all five fingers. "Someone in shipping and receiving at Discount Mart." My white hand's in the air like a creepy clown's glove. "I know you don't want to include anyone at Discount Mart, Lacey, but we have to cover all the bases."

"What happens at night here?" Junie asks.

"We lock up," Lacey says.

I pick at the flaky glue on my hand. "As in, secure?" I get an edge and pull. Yay. This white glue is the best medical invention since bubble-gum-flavored anti-biotics.

"Yeah, it's secure. Like everybody's. Watch, I'll show you." Lacey points to where a thin metal wall rolls down from the top of the kiosk. "See this lock? I have a key for that. And the product stays behind the barrier."

Junie jiggles the barrier.

We exchange looks. "Someone could break in pretty easily," I say.

"They lock up the mall about an hour after closing time," Lacey says.

"So we need to add that hour to the potential tampering time," Junie says.

A couple of guys in oversized Chaparral High

131

School T-shirts saunter up. Hands in the pockets of their sagging shorts, they stand, shuffling their feet. His eyes fixed on a row of packages of fake lashes and nails, one of them says, "Hey, like, it's our girl-friends' birthdays. And they, like, sorta want some makeup from here."

Lacey and Amber morph into selling mode with questions about hair and eye color and clothing choices. You couldn't tell by watching them that they're in the middle of a cosmetics crisis with an investigation that's going round and round like a Halloween corn maze. Well, maybe you could tell if you looked closely at Lacey, who's paler and less focused than usual, with a wrinkle that's starting to make itself at home on her forehead.

I finish stripping the dregs of glue from between my fingers, then retrieve my backpack and denim purse. "Wanna go see what Crystal has to say about Eve?" Junie never did get to check out Eve earlier, thanks to my disaster with the basket of lotion + a pair of wedge sandals.

"Sure, but I don't have long. Nick and his mom are meeting me at the food court. She's going to drive us to the Upscale Coffee Shop to catch the Detours playing."

Nick likes the Detours? Very weird. They're one of my favorite bands.

Arm in arm, Junie and I tramp up the stairs to the department store.

At the department store, Crystal's in charge of four different counters, each featuring a different brand of makeup. All the girls who work there are part-time, except for Crystal. The part-time girls handle sales at a couple of the counters, but Crystal allowed Amber to work all the counters. Because Amber is *that* good; she can sell to anyone.

When we get there, Crystal's on the phone with her back to us. But Suze, who works part-time at the Guy Mardi counter, spots us and waves us over.

Everything about Suze is short: her height, her hair, her skirt. According to Amber, Suze was pretty devastated when Amber quit to work at Naked Makeup. Even though they can easily meet in the food court for lunch. Anyway, Suze's always friendly to Junie and me and generous with samples. "Hi, guys, how's Amber doing?"

"Good," we say.

Probably she's asking because Crystal told her about Naked Makeup's sad scenario. Given how tight the makeup world is and all.

From beneath her counter, Suze pulls out a bunch of little packets. "The Guy Mardi rep came by yesterday. We have a brand-new line, Automne, coming out in the fall. Gorgeous colors. Here's some eye shadow and gloss." She scoots the packets to-ward us.

Junie and I look at each other. Normally we would've jumped on those samples like a half-off sale at Sequin's, but we're both sort of spooked by cos-metics at the moment. Yikes. We're becoming Janes by default.

"Oh, uh, thanks," I say, sweeping them into my purse, where they'll disappear into the black hole of blue denim.

"We want to talk with Crystal," Junie says.

"She should be off the phone soon. She's been talk-ing to the head office in Montreal for a while. Sounds like she's trying to arrange a trip up there."

"Ooh la la." I like to toss out a little French when-ever I can.

"Montreal's in Canada," Suze says. "Where they speak Eskimo."

"French Canada." Junie rocks at geography.

Junie taps her watch and raises her eyebrows at me. To Suze, she says, "We're looking for a girl named Eve. She came for a job interview today."

Suze's leaning on the glass counter, filing her thumbnail.

"She didn't end up coming in." Suze blows nail dust into the air. "She got a job at Pets Galore."

Junie and I gallop out of Crystal's makeup depart-ment before she even realizes we were there.

Junie skips off merrily to the food court to meet up with Nick and his mom.

I give The Ruler a quick call to let her know I'm okay. Then I'm headed to Pets Galore to track down the mysterious Eve.

chapter
nineteen

Pushing open the heavy glass door, I exit the fateful main entrance of the mall, take the sidewalk to the street, cross at the light, then wend my way through the parking lot to one of my fave stores of all time, Pets Galore.

Ahhh. I inhale deeply. Pets Galore is a happy place, filled with a delightful smell of fish food + dog grooming + birds. I could spend hours here.

Troy, the cashier, is an older guy of at least twenty-five. Tattoos of sea animals swim up and down his arms. All bright and cheerful, he says, "Hi, Sherry. How're Cindy and Prince?"

"Great. Zipping around their tank like crazy." I hike my backpack and my purse up onto my shoulder. I am heavily laden today. "Hey, Troy, did a girl named Eve just start working here?"

"Yeah." He's slotting the new pet magazines in the rack. "She's here now."

And then I smell something else. An odor that so does not belong in a pet shop. Cinnabon rolls. It's getting stronger and sweeter. It's Mrs. Howard. She's checking up on me.

My only advantage is that she doesn't know I can smell her. Which means she doesn't know that I know she's there. My foot midair, I do an about-face, stick my hands casually in my pockets and smile like a typical shopper, not a detective. By the time she knows about this mystery, it'll be signed, sealed and delivered to her at Dairy Queen.

"So, Troy, remember the castle I bought here that you recommended? Prince and Cindy love, love, love it. Got any new aquarium stuff?"

"A few plastic plants. Not sure they're your style, though." Now he's hanging little bags of catnip. "We just got a new bridge. Your fish might like that."

"I bet they would. Cindy and Prince don't have anything bridgelike. Thanks." I meander over to the fish aisle.

The Cinnabon smell trails after me.

I spot the new plants stacked on a shelf. Troy's right. They aren't worth saving up for. But I take my time examining them, turning them this way and that, holding them up close, then at arm's length. I move to the middle of the aisle and find the bridge. It's übercute. For a sec, I forget about the mystery and Mrs. Howard following me around and imagine Cindy and Prince darting under this little ceramic bridge. Until I turn it over and see the price tag. Ouchie mama! It's more than two weeks' allowance!

Mrs. Howard materializes beside me, big and round and hazy.

My hand on my heart, I stumble backward in fake shock. I swivel my head back and forth, making sure no one's around. "Mrs. Howard?" I whisper.

"Sorry to startle you, honey," she whispers back. Which she doesn't need to do since no one can hear her but me.

"Is my mom okay?"

"Honey, your mama's just grand. And making everyone real proud with the way she's focusing and learning. By everyone, I mean us *and* the prestigious foreign Academy. If things keep on progressing this a-way, your mama will get an exciting assignment, and we'll get to borrow one of their members."

Voices! And they're getting louder! A girl employee strides toward where I'm standing. A woman follows her.

"We have a pretty good selection of aquarium decorations." The girl stops right beside me.

I look at her badge. Eve!

Mrs. Howard drifts to the ceiling.

The woman's gazing at the various castles and treasure chests and colored pebbles. "He doesn't have anything in his aquarium yet." She looks at Eve. "What's your best seller? I have no idea what to buy."

She hesitates. Because she's brand-new, she can't offer much aquarium assistance!

My natural helpfulness kicks in. "A lot of people go for this castle." I point to a medieval castle with a few turrets. "But, personally, I prefer this castle." I hand the merchandise to the customer. "Yes, it's two dollars more. But see how it's got bigger swim-through chambers? My fish are constantly playing tag because of them."

"Swim-through chambers. I never would've thought of that." She holds the castle up to the light. "This'll be perfect."

"Eve, customer at crickets," the loudspeaker cuts in. "Eve, you're needed at crickets."

"That's for me. Is there anything else?" Eve looks at the woman, who shakes her head. "Thanks," Eve says to me, then jogs down the aisle.

As soon as we're alone again, Mrs. Howard descends. "Sherry, you can be such a polite, helpful young lady."

"Yeah, well, I am into fish."

"How gratifying to see you exhibiting exemplary behavior." Mrs. Howard floats close to my ear. "I want to pass along a little insider info I received from a snitch. The foreign Academy will be nosing around this week, watching your behavior, making sure you aren't a potential embarrassment either to our Academy or to your mother. Please be more than extra careful with your conduct. . . ."

I give her a thumbs-up. "No worries, Mrs. H."

And *poof,* she and her Cinnabon smell are gone.

I shake my head. So, a bunch of foreign ghosts will be spying on me. How creepy is that? But it makes me more determined than ever to get to the bottom of the makeup tampering so I can prove that I deserve a special assignment with my mom. And Real Time too.

I jaunt over to the crickets.

"Twenty-five, right?" I hear Eve's voice before I see her.

Rounding the corner, I see a blond boy about Sam's age, his head bobbing as Eve taps crickets from a tube into a clear plastic bag.

"Yeah. They're for my veiled chameleon, Frank. He's eating a lot. Probably getting ready to shed."

Holding the bag closed at the top, Eve starts counting under her breath. She shakes her head and starts over. Finally, she shrugs, blows air into the bag, then knots it shut. "I'm sure there are a few extra." She hands the bag to the boy, then turns to me, "Oh, hi. Something I can help you with?"

I wait till the boy's out of sight, then frown like I'm trying to place her. "You look familiar. Did you used to work at the mall or something?"

"For like a month. At Naked Makeup."

"That is trippy makeup."

"Seriously."

"So, you worked for Lacey?" I glance in the cricket box, acting all nonchalant.

"You know her?"

"Kinda. I just had a makeover slumber party. And I got a bunch of makeup from her." Now I'm examining the reptile lamps. "I wish I could work there. Except I'm only thirteen."

"It's a good job." She pops open the lid to the cricket container and spoons in some orange jellylike food. "Depending on what you want to do in life."

"What do you mean?"

"Like I want to work with animals, so Pets Galore'll look better on my résumé. My parents and I just visited Tucson over the weekend to look at the pre-vet program there and the profs liked that I was working here."

If Eve was in Tucson for the weekend, she wasn't tampering with makeup at the Phoenix Mall. Besides, anyone who likes animals enough to be a vet must be cool.

"Are they pretty nice to you here?" I ask. "As nice as Lacey?"

"This is only my first day, but no complaints on my end." She straightens the tubs of wax worms. "Of course, Lacey's super super nice. Everyone likes her. Discount Mart especially loves her. They've been fantastic about adjusting her hours so she can get her makeup business off the ground." She stacks the egg cartons. "And then there's that one guy."

My detective ears perk up. "What one guy?"

"Eve, customer needs assistance in dog food," the loudspeaker crackles. "Eve to dog food."

"What one guy?" I repeat. Goose bumps pop up all over my arms.

"I don't know. Just some Discount Mart shipping and receiving guy who's always texting and sending her flowers."

chapter
twenty

I'm out in the fresh Arizona air, jetting home for dinner. I hope it's yummy, because I've worked up a mammoth appetite with all this sleuthing.

I call Amber. When she picks up, I say, "I need Lacey's number."

"She's right beside me. I'll pass her my phone."

In half a sec, Lacey's on the line. "Did you already figure out who's messing with my makeup?"

"Uh, not yet. Lacey, is there a shipping and receiving guy at Discount Mart who's crushing on you?"

She sighs. "Drew. He's nice and all, but just not my type."

"Don't you have the makeup sent to Discount Mart?"

"Yeah. Drew sets my shipments to the side for me and keeps an eye on them."

I want to reach through the phone and slap some sense into her. Doesn't she get it? *Everyone* who's involved with Naked Makeup is a potential suspect. "Any reason why Drew might sabotage the makeup?"

"No, no, no. He's a total sweetheart. Just kind of nerdy."

"Does he know you don't like him the way he likes you?"

"Uh, probably. Since I'm constantly refusing to go out with him."

A little lightbulb flashes on in my head. "The fresh-cut flowers you always have by the cash register? Are they from him?"

She sighs again. "I keep telling him to stop."

"So, he buys you flowers, but you won't go out with him. And he's still okay with keeping your packages safe?"

"Well, yeah," Lacey says. "He wants me to succeed with Naked Makeup."

"For sure? He actually says this?"

"Well, no, he doesn't say it exactly like that. More like he says he doesn't want me to quit Discount Mart because then he wouldn't see me," Lacey says. "But I'm positive he wants Naked Makeup to take off even if it means I'll leave Discount Mart. He's a good guy. He wants what I want."

"Maybe, in reality, he wants to wreck your business so you're stuck working at Discount Mart, near him, for the rest of your life. That's called motive." I want to scream at her. "And he could easily contaminate the makeup while he's 'keeping it safe'"—I make air quotes—"then package it back up good as new with Discount Mart tape and staples and whatever. That's called opportunity. And those two things, motive and opportunity, are all you need for a crime."

"I don't think Drew'd do all that," Lacey says. "It's so, uh, so twisted."

"Yeah, Lacey, that's why they call it twisted love." I disconnect, shaking my head.

My foot is barely in the door when The Ruler calls out, "Sherry, could you please take your brother around the neighborhood while I finish making dinner?"

Sam bounces up to me. "My wagon's packed." *Bounce, bounce.* "You just have to walk with me." *Bounce, bounce.* "It's cabbage casserole for dinner." *Bounce, bounce.*

"Fine, but quit the Tigger routine, you're exhausting me." I drop my backpack and purse by the door. "Let's hit the road."

"Be careful you don't hurt yourself."

I groan. Apparently, my brother shares my dad's bad-pun habit.

We pass through the kitchen, where The Ruler's tossing a salad. The casserole is obviously bubbling away in the oven because the cabbage fumes are practically knocking me unconscious. However, if you can get past the smell, cabbage casserole is *el delicioso*. It's got this to-die-for cheesy sauce with walnuts and tofu. In a million years, I never thought I'd crave anything health-foodish, but there's something about The Ruler's cooking.

In the garage, Sam's wagon is all loaded up with stuff he and The Ruler have been growing in our backyard: tomatoes, carrots, celery, beets and prickly pear cacti. My hands start itching at the sight of the evil cacti and their nasty bristles. He's also got brown paper bags and a little box with some change in it. My brother got enough organization genes for the two of us. Even his sock drawer is all nice and neat with the contents paired up.

We trudge to the end of the driveway with Sam pulling the wagon. One of the wheels is squeaking. I think it's saying, "Go home. Eat dinner." My stomach grumbles.

"Left or right?" I ask.

"What do you think, Sherry?" he says. "Which way will I get the most sales?"

I seriously don't think he's going to sell much

146

regardless of the direction. Especially not those ugly beets that look bruised and purple, like they've been in a knock-down, drag-out garden fight. "Go right. It's less hilly."

"Good idea, Sherry."

Well, I am the big sister. "Sam, I noticed you don't have a calculator. You can borrow my phone. It has one under Tools."

"Thanks, Sherry." He yanks on the wagon handle to get it started. "I can just add in my head."

I know he's supposed to be some kind of math whiz, but I think he's pushing it, especially 'cause we're talking about money. A small mistake with a decimal point could spell financial ruin.

When we get to the driveway of our closest neighbor, I say, "No point trying Mrs. Moore. She's such a grump. Plus she's got that No Solicitors sign on her front door."

Sam keeps tramping up her drive. "She's also got a sign that says Guard Dog/Beware of Dog and we know that's a lie."

At the front steps, he passes me the handle to hold and walks to the door. He presses the bell.

A thin face with a hook nose peers out the window. Then I hear the dead bolt moving and the front door cracks open. "Yes?"

"Hi, Mrs. Moore. It's Sam from next door." He points to the wagon. "I've been growing organic plants in our garden and now I'm going door to door, selling them." He lists his wares.

She squints down the steps to the wagon. "Which sports team are you on?"

"Oh, uh, no sports team," Sam says. "I'm just saving up to buy some stuff, special stuff."

"No sports team?" She shakes her head vigorously but her tight steel gray curls barely budge. They're hair-sprayed into submission. "Good for you, Sam. I don't believe in sports teams. Makes kids too competitive. Turns them into bullies."

She totters down the steps, her heels slipping out of the backs of her fuzzy slippers. "What're you saving up for?" she asks, weighing a tomato in each of her palms.

"It's a secret." Sam smiles and unfolds a bag for her.

"A secretive boy who doesn't play sports." She places a bunch of carrots in a bag, then sets the tomatoes in carefully. "I like it." She even buys a couple of beets.

We set off down the road, both of us tugging on the handle. A brother, a sister, a squeaky wagon and a bunch of produce. Sam's whistling in his normal too-high-pitched, tuneless way. Usually it bugs me to death, but this evening I'm glad for the familiar sound. We're in that comfortable sibling place where we don't feel like talking but we're getting along fine.

Somewhere between Mr. Scott's and the Dixon

family's house, I smell coffee. Mom! She doesn't say anything, just whooshes along next to us. Sam seems unaware, as usual, of my mother's presence. I'm the only one who can talk with her, occasionally feel her, smell her, but I never see her. A brother, a sister and a mother out for a walk at dusk. It's weird, but it's a way the three of us can hang together.

Finally, when Sam's up doing his sales pitch to the Dixons and can't hear us, she sighs. "This is the kind of stuff I miss, Sherry. Just being with you guys."

"Me too."

"You two seem to be doing okay, though." She sighs again. "Paula's really looking after you. And I'm so grateful for that. She's doing things for you that I can't." Mom moves right beside me. The coffee scent is strong, like I'm in the coffee aisle at the grocery store.

"She is taking care of us, Mom, but it's not like she's replacing you. Don't ever think that." My bangs lift ever so slightly and I feel a light touch across my forehead. I close my eyes and just feel.

"Sherry! Sherry!" Sam's hopping down the Dixons' steps. "They want six tomatoes!"

After he takes care of the transaction and the three of us are a ways down the road, I see my brother suck in a small breath and cock his head slightly to the side. He smiles. He doesn't know it's Mom, but he must sense enough to know it's love.

She stays with us until everything from the wagon is sold. Even the beets.

Sam and I plod back home. Dinner is super yummy. Plus, all that exercise right before the meal really got my appetite going. After my last bite, I undo the snap on my jeans. The Ruler heads down the hall to do some grading in our little office.

My dad and Sam launch into one of their fave activities. This is exchanging dumber-than-dumb knock-knock jokes.

"Knock, knock," Sam says.

"Who's there?" Dad says.

"Interrupting cow."

"Interrupting c—"

"Mooo!" Sam's grabbing his stomach, doubled over with laughter.

Sadly, so is my dad.

I roll my eyes. "I'm going to hit the books."

"Don't hurt your—"

I plug my ears. "Please, Dad, don't embarrass yourself."

I leave the room to the sound of my brother and my father busting up like maniacs.

I'm sprawled all over my bed, finishing my math homework. I add a negative sign to my answer, slam the textbook shut, lean back on my pillow, grab my phone and speed-dial Josh.

"Hi, Sherry!"

Basically, my insides go all oatmealy when I hear his voice. It doesn't matter that I saw him earlier today. I could've seen him five seconds ago, and still his voice would do that to me. Love is one strange state.

"What'd you do after school?" I ask.

"Swim team, then I helped my dad with some landscaping junk," Josh says. "How about you?"

I fill him in on the lotion + bristles. And how I've booted Eve out of the suspect pool. "We still have Wacko Will. Then there's the Janes at school. You know, that bizarro group of girls who won't wear makeup and don't want anyone else to either."

"Nah, I don't really know anything about them," Josh says.

"Your cousin Kim's one of them."

"Yeah, well, Kim's always been kind of weird. But harmless. Like, last year, she didn't want any Christmas presents. She wanted us to donate money to a cause. We bought a tree in her name in the rain forest."

"That *is* weird." Although it sounds like a gift The Ruler would go for. I tuck the thought away. "Kim probably is completely harmless, but that doesn't mean all the Janes are."

"You think the Janes might be trying to convince lots of people to boycott makeup by ruining Naked Makeup's reputation?"

"Yeah, maybe. I mean, Naked Makeup's getting pretty popular and it's already super super popular with teens."

"Any other suspects?" Josh asks.

"A guy we haven't checked out yet." I tell him about Drew and his crazy crush on Lacey. "I'm going over to Discount Mart tomorrow after school to see what vibes I get from him in person."

"Hey, I'll go with you."

"You are so on."

Because what could be better than investigating with your boyfriend?

chapter
twenty-one

I t's Tuesday after school, and I'm in The Ruler's car, tagging along with her and Sam to Grandma Baldwin's. Not because I want to help with the horrendous bird chore. Not because I want to listen to Grandma's new age craziness. Not because I want to watch her favor Sam over me.

No, no, no. There's only one reason why I'm headed to Grandma Baldwin's. I need to make contact with Grandpa.

By nature, The Ruler's a snail-like driver. She hunches over the steering wheel, the only time she ever slouches, crawling away from stop signs. We'll be lucky to make it to Grandma's before Thanksgiving.

"It's so great you're coming with me." Sam looks up from his video game and beams. "There's a ton of bird work."

I groan inwardly. Because of the flock of cactus wrens flying overhead when Grandpa died, Grandma now sees herself as grand pooh-bah protector of all birds on earth. She doesn't realize that Grandpa chills in her backyard, eating her out of pounds of sunflower seeds, waiting for the day she clues in to his identity.

The Ruler relaxes and straightens up as we exit Phoenix and motor along less crowded streets. The traffic thins down to nothing as we approach the nowheresville my grandmother calls home.

Finally, The Ruler turns off a bumpy potholed road and onto the bumpy potholed driveway. She jerks to a stop by Grandma's porch. Sam and I clamber out.

Grandma is through her creaky screen door and down her wooden front steps before you can say, "Welcome to the country." She grabs Sam and me up in a tight herbalish hug, then clomps to The Ruler's open window. "I just made some iced mango tea. Can you come in and visit?"

"Maybe later." The Ruler keeps glancing in the rearview mirror, trying to gauge a backing-up strategy. Reverse isn't her strong suit. "I have some shopping to do at the co-op."

Grandma grabs our hands, and Sam and I climb up ths steps. We walk beneath the ceramic sun centered above the front door, entering the house of new age bizarreness.

Over my shoulder, I see The Ruler inching down the drive.

In the kitchen, Grandma passes me a long-handled wooden spoon and parks me in front of the stove and a humongous pot. "Sherry, you're in charge of sugar water for the hummingbird feeders. All you have to do is stir."

"Am I making food for the entire Western Hemisphere?"

Sam giggles.

Grandma frowns. "Sam, let's get some bags of seed from the shed."

I prop the spoon in the pot. "I'll help with that." I gotta find Grandpa.

"The birds aren't used to you the way they are to Sam," Grandma says. "It'd be less distracting if you stayed inside while we're filling the feeders."

Ack. Eek. Ike. I can't be stuck in the kitchen. I absolutely have to talk to Grandpa about helping me with the mystery.

"Grandma, they're wild birds, not pets. It doesn't matter if they're not used to me."

"That shows how little you understand," she says like I'm in kindergarten. "Tell her about the wren,

Sam. The wren that follows me everywhere, that eats sunflower seeds from my hands, that rides on my shoulder."

It's Grandpa! I want to shout.

"Seriously, Sherry," Sam says, "it's almost like he's talking to Grandma."

He *is* talking to Grandma!

Grandma clutches the tiny crystal that hangs from a chain around her wrist. "One day, I swear he said my name. Mary Ann. It was very clear." She pauses. "Well, it wasn't that clear. It was the way a bird beak would say my name."

"Like this?" I imitate Grandpa's croaky, garbled voice. "Maaary Aaaannn."

Her wrinkly jaw drops. "That's exactly what he sounded like."

"Maaary Aaaannn," I rasp out again.

"Have you met him?" Only my grandmother can ask a question like that and think it's somehow normal.

"I've seen him around." Actually, I could list a bunch of places where I've hung out with Grandpa, but one look at Sam, who's contemplating me like a science textbook, and I stop. I can't risk breaking the Academy rule of secrecy. Especially right now, when I'm supposed to be on my best behavior. And, with Sam, you never know what he'll put together.

Sometimes, I think he's Einstein genius. Other times, he's just my nerdy, annoying little brother.

Grandma unhooks her bracelet. "You take this, Sherry." She drops it in my palm. "It's citrine, a type of quartz that's helpful for skin disorders in animals."

I paste a puzzled look on my face, but I know exactly what she's referring to. Grandpa's little head is all balding and his feather coverage is patchy, especially over his protruding tummy. Grandma thinks the stone will help his condition.

"I haven't been able to get him to wear this." Her gnarled hands on my shoulders, she gives me a little squeeze. "Why don't you try?"

My eyebrows jump up. "Grandma, you seriously think he'll wear this?"

"Even if it just stays around his neck for a few minutes to start." Her eyes are pleading.

Why am I arguing? I want a chance to track down Grandpa. Plus, this'll put me in Grandma's good graces.

"Okeydokey." I tap out a little victory tune on the counter with the spoon. "I'm your girl, then."

Sam pushes open the porch door.

Grandma's backyard is, uh, different. It's dotted all over with birdhouses, birdbaths and saguaro cacti. Hummingbird feeders hang from palm trees, as do two-liter plastic soda bottles that have been converted into feeders, and giant pinecones rolled first in peanut butter, then bird seed. Of course, with all this paraphernalia to attract birds, there's a fair amount of bird poop around. In short, it's the backyard of a woman obsessed with birds.

We stand in the middle of all this birdness, blinking in the bright southwestern sun.

"He loves sunflower seeds," Grandma says. "I usually fill the feeder next to the giant saguaro with nothing but sunflower seeds for him."

We wander in that direction. I spot Grandpa first. He's perched on an arm of a cactus, his head tucked under his ratty wing. He's got a little snore going. I open my mouth to call out, "Grandpa," then snap it shut.

"There he is," Sam shouts.

Grandpa wakes up with a snort.

"Yoo-hoo, John Wayne!" Grandma crooks a finger.

"John Wayne?" I say. "The old actor in bad westerns?"

"I've always had a thing for cowboys." She puts a hand over her heart.

Grandpa flaps up to a higher arm of the cactus.

Grandma's face falls.

"Hey, birdie, birdie," I say, "this stone will help you grow a bunch of feathers."

"Sherry," Grandpa says. "No rock."

He crosses his wings.

"Is he talking to you?" Sam asks.

I shoot him a withering big-sister look. "Get real."

Grandma stands right next to me. "John Wayne, this is my granddaughter, Sherry. She's usually a pretty good girl. Come meet her.

"Sam, run to the shed and get the large bag of sunflower seeds," Grandma instructs. "We'll sprinkle a ring of them around your sister. That'll get John Wayne down."

The sec Sam takes off, I say, "Grandma, maybe if I had a moment alone with, uh, John Wayne? Then it wouldn't look like we're all ganging up on him."

"Brilliant, Sherry. I'll work on the sugar water in the kitchen." Grandma disappears down a row of birdhouses. For an old lady, she can scamper when she wants to.

Grandpa is really tough for me to understand, although my mom doesn't have any trouble. "Übermuffled" is the word that leaps to mind. I gotta keep this convo simple.

"Grandpa, come here," I say in a loud whisper. "We need to talk."

"No."

"It's not about the rock." I hang the bracelet on a low cactus arm. It dangles and spins and gleams.

"Although, couldn't you just, like, rub your head on it or something? It would make Grandma *super* happy."

"Fine."

"Thank you," I say. "Really I'm here because I need help."

In a flash, he's on my head.

"There's a mystery at the Phoenix Mall. Mom can't help. 'Cause of all that hush-hush foreign Academy stuff."

"What?" he squawks.

Oops. "Not important, not important."

Sam arrives with a wheelbarrow. Inside slumps the hugest plastic bag of sunflower seeds ever.

"Yum," Grandpa croaks.

"He's on your head!" Sam drops the handles, and the barrow clunks down.

"Where I don't want him to stay." I point to the seed. "Pour some of that on the ground."

With his teeth, Sam bites a hole in the end of the bag hanging over the barrow, then wheels a circle around me, leaving a trail of seeds.

"Sherry, how's it going?" Grandma calls out.

"Give me a few more minutes," I shout. "Take the rest of that seed back to the shed," I tell Sam.

Grandpa's munching up a storm, eating his way around the circle.

"Mrs. Howard won't assign Mom to the mystery." I

hunker down close so I can talk quietly. "She doesn't even want me to work on it."

Seed spilling out of his beak, Grandpa peers up at me. "Bossy lady."

"So will you help me investigate someone?"

"Yes."

"He *is* talking to you!" Sam steps out from where he was crouching under a birdbath.

chapter
twenty-two

Feet shoulder-width apart and arms crossed, Sam stares at me. "You were definitely asking that bird questions. And it was definitely answering."

Now that the seeds are gone, Grandpa flaps off.

"Did Grandma see?" I ask, making my voice all hopeful. I can't let Sam figure out the bird's true identity. I can't be responsible for revealing another Academy secret. I have to convince him the whole talking-with-a-bird routine was an act to impress Grandma.

"What?"

"I really wanted Grandma to see."

Sam's arms drop to his sides.

"I don't think she did. I think she was in the kitchen the whole time," I say. "Could you tell her?"

"I guess. Sure. Why?" He's überconfused.

"I want her to believe I was connecting with her special bird."

"What?"

"Of course I was asking the bird questions, but there's no way the bird was answering. Sam, don't be a moron. It's a bird. It was doing what birds do, pecking and squawking and bobbing its head."

"So you were faking it? Asking the bird questions just to impress Grandma?" Sam's got a sudoku look on his face. As in, he's concentrating hard, trying to make sense of this whole scenario.

"Exactly."

"Why?"

"Just for once," I say, "I want to be her favorite."

"What?"

"She's liked you best for forever. I want a turn. And if she thinks I'm in with her feathered friend, I'll earn tons of granddaughter points."

He shakes his head like I'm loony tunes. "She doesn't have a favorite."

Which is exactly what people who are the favorite always think.

When we get to the kitchen, Grandma's in there pouring mango tea for The Ruler.

She's explaining the whole citrine quartz + favorite wren + baldness and general skin-disorder thing until The Ruler's eyes glaze over.

"I think it'll work," Sam says. "Sherry was getting through to the bird."

Grandma envelops me in a big hug. "I knew you could do it, Sherry. You have such a strong, clean aura."

Sam winks at me.

I punch him softly on the arm. I would feel guilty about lying, but I'm able to totally rationalize it. If I keep my behavior squeaky clean and solve the makeup mystery, the Academy will love me and give me loads of Real Time. Which I'll share with Sam.

An arm around each of us, Grandma walks Sam and me to the front door. She's yakking away about how balanced my energy chakras are. Apparently, I'm in complete and total harmony.

While I'm in Grandma's crystalish good graces, I toss free beauty advice her way. "Grandma, have you considered using cosmetics? I could come over one day and give you a complete makeover. I'm even an expert with face shapes."

Silence.

"With all-natural products, of course," I add. "I could do your hair too. Untangle that gray braid you've got going and try a new style."

"I would like that, Sherry." There's a catch in Grandma's voice.

Maybe she's been wanting to beautify herself for years and was just waiting for someone to show an interest. Maybe she's been waiting for me.

"We could hit a shoe store too. And pick you out some pretty footwear." I doubt clunky hippie sandals were ever in style.

"The Birkenstocks stay," Grandma says firmly.

I glance over my shoulder to see The Ruler quietly pouring her drink down the sink drain.

We're driving home. Sluggishly. The Ruler's knuckles are white where she's gripping the steering wheel.

Sam's imitating me imitating Grandpa by repeating over and over in a hoarse voice, "Maaary Aaannn. Maaary Aaannn."

It's time to ramp up the investigation. It's time to do something really tough that totally goes against my nature: infiltrate the Janes. They are nutzoid enough to go after the makeup that's rapidly becoming the most popular makeup in our school. Which means I have to be nutzoid enough to go after them.

I text Brianna.

```
<u still in the janes?>
<yeah. u gonna join?>
```

<maybe>
<pls join. i need the points>
<wat?>
<bec im new i have 0 points. so im the
water girl. i have 2 buy all the bottled
water for the mtg. they drink tons! 2
keep skin clear naturally>
<ill get bak to u>

I do not want to be water girl for that club of
freaks.
I text Junie.

<wat u doing?>
<homework>
<josh's gonna help me check out drew @
discount mart>
<cool>
<wat abt the janes? we need 2 infiltrate>
<no>
<no wat?>
<no im not joining the janes>
<but im investigating drew>
<im already in the latin club. ur not in
any clubs>
<the latin club doesnt count>
<i cant give up makeup. remember my
face? which u did 2 me>

<junie!!!>
<no. besides they really want u to join.
ull be like a hero there>

I think of how they surrounded me like I was a
wounded animal on the African savanna, and they
were hungry hyenas. Victim is more like what I'd be.

<theyll eat me alive>
<dont b so drama queen. u join tomorrow.
bye>

Ack! Me. School. Makeupless. Ack!

chapter
twenty-three

I am a nervous wreck all day Wednesday at school. Sweaty hands, rapid heartbeat, difficulty concentrating.

Every chance I get, I sneak off to the restroom to reapply my lip gloss, mascara, eye shadow and blush. I'm getting my makeup fixes while I can because today, after school, I'm doing the unthinkable. I'm joining the Janes.

After the last class, I text Josh to meet me at the big stone saguaro cactus statue in the courtyard. He's there before me, all cool and relaxed, leaning against the statue. His jeans are loose and baggy and his T-shirt's loose and baggy too. My heart does a major flip.

He locks me in a hug and I snuggle into the comforting smells of chlorine and laundry soap. If only I could stay here forever, safe and sound and with my lip gloss shiny and thick. But no, there's a case, and it's up to me to crack it.

I pull away. "Josh, I'm joining the Janes. For the mystery. I have to know what they're up to. And if it includes contaminating Naked Makeup products."

"Okay."

"Josh, I don't think you understand what I'm saying. I'm joining the Janes. Today. In, like, five minutes."

"Okay."

"Josh." I keep my voice even and patient even though I want to scream because he's obviously not getting the seriousness of the situation. "I have to hand in the rest of my makeup. They already got what I keep in my backpack."

"Oh, I see." He smiles and musses up my hair. "Sherry Holmes Baldwin, you always look great to me."

My boy is so the best.

Josh's phone vibrates. He checks the screen. "Eric's wondering why I'm not at swim practice." He leans over and his lips brush against mine. "The Janes won't know what hit them with you in the club." And he lopes off to the pool.

I plod to the restroom. After a few deep breaths, I

wet a paper towel and, with shaky hands, get to work removing every inch of my makeup.

When I'm done, I stare in the mirror. Staring back at me is the face of a pale but serious detective. A detective who's going deep undercover. A detective who can say, "I so don't do makeup."

I tromp over to room eleven and tug on the doorknob. Locked. I peer in through the little rectangular window. A bunch of girls, more than I would've expected for such a sketchy club, are sitting at desks, their eyes trained on Jane #1, aka Emily, at the front of the class. No one's smiling. They all look super serious. And anemic.

I knock. My heart pounds. I so don't want to do this.

The door swings open. "Tardiness is not tolerated." Staring at me is a round face with minor acne that could easily be covered by concealer. "Wow! Wow!" The Jane spins around, whipping her frizzy shoulder-length hair in my face. "Everybody! Everybody!" She points a colorless nail at me. "It's her! She's here!"

Brianna hops out of her chair and rushes over to give me a hug. "Thank you so much, Sherry. I owe you." She raises my arm in the air. "She's mine, guys. I mean, Janes. I talked her into coming. I get the points."

"You're really joining?" Kim asks, her voice heavy with doubt.

"Of course she's joining," Brianna snaps. "And I'm not buying one more bottle of water for you people. Not one more."

Jane #1 marches up to me and shakes my hand, pumping my arm with enthusiasm. "Welcome to your future, Sherry. You're making a very wise choice."

I smile weakly. I honestly can't think of an answer. I massage my shoulder when she finally lets go.

The Janes form a line that snakes around the perimeter of the classroom. Jane #1 stands beside me, next to the door, as each girl shakes my hand to welcome me to the club. It's a freakish version of a receiving line at a wedding. Minus the bride and the groom and the wedding party. And cute clothes. And romantic makeup.

At the end of the line, stands Jane #2, aka Tess. Hands on her hips, she says, "Hand it over, Sherry."

I sigh. From my backpack, I slide out a Ziploc bag of makeup. I open the bag and inhale deeply, then whisper a quiet goodbye. I close my eyes.

Jane #2 rips the bag from my hands.

The Janes clap.

I feel sick. Yes, it's my oldest, least favorite makeup. But there are memories associated with it.

Everyone files back to their seats. Jane #1 indicates an empty desk in the far right row, near the middle of the room. With a little head swiveling, I have a good view of everyone.

Jane #1 trots to the front of the room and resumes the meeting. "Sherry, we're planning a demonstration for next Monday in the school courtyard before classes."

"I think we should each carry a sign proclaiming our future profession," Jane #2 says.

"I'll print handouts," says the round-faced, acned Jane who opened the door. "So everyone understands we're not anti-makeup, but *pro*-potential."

"Let's have wipes handy for any girls who are so moved they want to remove their makeup right on the spot," another Jane says.

"I'll bring a trash can for girls to throw out their makeup," Kim says.

"We should wear matching T-shirts."

"Maybe we can recruit from other middle schools too."

Great ideas? Yeah, if you're planning a demonstration at an old folks' home. No way these are the real plans. The Janes aren't tricking me. Not that I've ever been involved in a demonstration, but The Ruler does keep the news on at home. So I know from TV that real-life demonstrations are all about placards and chanting and throwing stones. Not about wipes and matching T-shirts.

The Janes must be keeping their biggest, scariest, most devastating plot of all secret. Probably they're afraid of revealing too much in front of a brand-new member. Such smart thinking isn't surprising from a group of girls who want to grow up to be lawyers and doctors and accountants.

Time for aggressive sleuthing that'll prod a Jane with a conscience to step forward with information.

Like illegal blast fishing, where you toss dynamite into a body of water and then scoop up the stunned fish, I will drop a bomb on the desk. What clues will float to the surface? This is the Discovery Channel meets crime discovery.

"Let's sabotage a bunch of product at Naked Makeup," I announce.

The Janes' jaws drop. Because they didn't realize I was onto them?

"We'll send a super strong message." I pound the desk with my fist. "'Wear makeup and you'll get hurt.'"

Their eyes flit back and forth. With guilt?

I stand and say in a loud voice, "We could add hot sauce to lip gloss and cactus spines to hand lotion."

The whole room is buzzing now.

And in the midst of the hubbub, my cell vibrates.

A text from Amber:

<Get over to the kiosk!>

chapter
twenty-four

I forward the text to Junie, then sneak out during the pandemonium.

Junie and I arrive at the kiosk at the same time, skidding to a sweaty stop in front of Amber. We look like we just ran the mile in PE. At least Junie's wearing makeup. All I've got going for me is my naturally long eyelashes.

"What's going on?" I say.

"Zero makeup, Sherry?" Amber says.

"I joined the Janes," I explain. "To spy."

She opens a drawer. "I'll fix you up."

"No! You can't." I cover my face. "The Janes probably have mall spies. If they report me, I'll be banned from Friday's meeting."

"Chill, Sherry." Amber closes the drawer with her hip. "It's not like I'm going to tie you to a chair and brush on eye shadow."

"What'd you do at the meeting?" Junie asks.

"I'll tell you later," I say. "Amber, what was the text about?"

Amber jerks a slender shoulder toward the other side of the kiosk. We walk around. Lacey's propped up on a stool. She has dark circles under her eyes that no amount of concealer could hide. Her hair is limp and lifeless. Her skin is pale and dry. She's überdepressed.

"Sales have slumped." Amber unwraps an energy bar. "A few shoppers came by today to say they won't be buying Naked Makeup anymore because it's too chancy. It's only a matter of time before the mall management gets wind of this and shuts down Lacey's business."

Lacey buries her sad head in her hands.

"Tell her how well the investigation is going." Amber breaks off the end of the energy bar and hands it to Lacey.

"Lacey, we're making incredible progress," I say in my perkiest of voices, which always works with Sam. "I've gone all out and even given up makeup. Which, yes, sounds like it doesn't make sense, but it was the only way to infiltrate the Janes."

"We have two other suspects as well," Junie says. "Will—"

"Ahem," I interrupt loudly and give her the hand-cut-across-the-neck signal to stop her, but, alas, Junie barrels on.

"And that Drew guy from Discount Mart."

Lacey jerks up her head. "It's not Drew."

"We're just being thorough," I explain. "It's the way we roll."

"Did you ever hear back from headquarters about the ingredients of Nite Sprite Creme?" Junie asks.

Lacey's head flops back down.

"It had a bunch of extra papaya acid in it." Amber snaps off more energy bar. "Like enough for a chemical peel that should've just been left on for three minutes. Think how much longer you guys left it on." She pops some bar in her mouth.

"Is it possible Naked Makeup put a Nite Sprite Creme label on a batch of chemical peel by mistake?" Junie asks.

"Naked Makeup doesn't make a chemical peel." Amber looks grim.

"I don't get how we kept sleeping with acid on our faces," Junie says. "We should've felt the itchiness and burning."

"There was a time-release formula in the cream," Lacey says all monotone, her head still down.

Yikes! We're lucky we have any faces left!

"Sherry, you gotta step it up with the investigation." Amber chews on the energy bar. "Crystal's coming over in a few. She has a really good idea to spark Naked Makeup sales."

We have this whole conversation without getting interrupted by a customer. So different from even a day ago.

Amber sends Junie and me over to the food court for a bottle of green tea for Lacey.

"Those makeup people really do look after each other," I say. "Green tea for Lacey? That's über-nurturing for Amber."

"And the way Crystal's coming over with makeup ideas for Lacey, who's basically a competitor?" Junie says. "Amber wasn't kidding when she described the makeup world as tight."

When we get back to the kiosk, Crystal's waiting in all her bling and glitter. She's dressed in a long fire-truck-red sequined T-shirt and a wide belt with a big shiny silver buckle. Metallic shadow accentuates her eyes, and she has the most adorable diamond stick-on by her left brow. She looks amazing and put to-gether and all Queen Sparkly of the Phoenix Mall. I practically need sunglasses to look at her.

Sigh. Which makes me more aware than ever that I'm makeupless.

Crystal looks at me and smiles. She's so tactful, she doesn't even mention my plainness. Not even the tiniest roll of her eyes.

I smile back. And to continue with my friendliness,

I ask, "So, did you get your trip to Montreal all planned?"

Amber screams.

Crystal turns the color of her T-shirt.

Amber grabs Crystal by the waist and dances her around. "You're going to Montreal? You got enough sales? Why didn't you tell me?"

"Uh, it's not totally a done deal yet." Crystal twists a stud earring.

"What's in Montreal?" Lacey asks.

"Only her dream job for Riley's Cosmetics," Amber says. Her emerald eyes flash with excitement. "Only what Crystal's been working toward for forever." She raises her hand for a high five. "You're finally getting out from behind the counter."

"I gotta show good sales growth over the next few weeks still." Crystal gives Amber a lackluster high five. Probably she's worried about jinxing herself. "How'd you hear about my trip?" she says to me.

"We stopped by your makeup counter," I say. "You were on the phone."

Lacey sips her tea. Amber brings Crystal up to speed on the suspect list.

Crystal dives into her brilliant save-Lacey's-business idea. "You need to attract customers in a new way. Ya gotta build up your clientele. I say offer classes."

Lacey slides off the stool and stands back from the

kiosk, her eyes flitting over her various bottles and jars and other containers. "We do carry a variety of products."

Amber is practically pogoing, she's so excited. "Saturday! Let's do it this Saturday! Seriously. We could do hair and faces and nails!"

"Hair!" Lacey perks right up, like she's stuck her finger in an electrical outlet. "Are you thinking what I'm thinking?"

"Hair Repair Extraordinaire!" they squeal in unison.

"Is it new?" Crystal asks.

"It is so brand-new," Amber says, "not all the vendors even stock it."

"We got a sample and then the opportunity to order it"—Lacey climbs on a footstool—"because our sales were through the roof." She goes still, then gives a little shake and opens a cupboard door.

"Drew called to let me know the shipment came in today." Lacey's rooting through the cupboard. "I'll pick it up at Discount Mart and bring it with me for the big event." Still on the stool, she turns around and waves a rectangular box with the standard Naked Makeup butterflies fluttering all over it. "You spray it on. Leave it in." Lacey snaps the fingers on her free hand. "And—"

"Presto!" Amber picks up. "Your hair is instantly frizzless, manageable and shiny."

"Incredible," Crystal says.

"It's a miracle," Amber says. "A Naked Makeup miracle."

"Let's call the event Fantabulous You!" Lacey's eyes sparkle. "And we'll set up twenty-minute appointments and work with four customers at a time. That's two for me and two for Amber." Her cheeks are pink with excitement. "I have so many ideas, I'm bursting with them." She hugs Crystal. "No wonder Riley's wants you in Montreal."

Clicking her tongue and deep in thought, Amber's staring at Junie and me.

I so do not like the look in her eyes.

chapter
twenty-five

Yay for boyfriends! Yay especially for Josh Morton! Who called me just as Amber was giving all kinds of boring chores to Junie and me so she and Lacey could get to work designing a flyer and tickets for Fantabulous You!

"Sherry, you know how you wanted me to go to Discount Mart with you?" Josh asks in his spine-tingling golden tones. "Can you go now? My mom's going shopping and could give us a ride."

"Right now?" I whine, like I'm being asked to do something responsible and boring. Meanwhile my heart's bouncing like a rubber ball.

"We could grab a slice of pizza and a soda for dinner there too," he says.

"Oh, fine, if I have to," I continue in whining mode.

"I thought you wanted me to help with the investigation," Josh says.

I turn my back to the kiosk. "I'm faking. So I don't look too anxious to get out of the work Amber gave me," I whisper into the phone. "I'm at the mall," I say loudly.

"Gotcha," he says. "Can my mom swing by the entrance by Movie World in ten minutes?"

"I guess," I say, sounding all resigned.

"Sherry, you crack me up." He disconnects.

I attempt to look serious and crestfallen, like maybe the call was from The Ruler, who's ordering me home for babysitting. "Sorry. Gotta blow this pop stand."

Junie glares at me because I'm sticking her with Amber's to-do list.

I mimic texting to let her know I'll be in touch.

Amber looks down her nose at me. "Junie can handle getting the flyers printed, but it'll take both of you to hand them out. Especially at your school."

"Uh, Amber? My cover? I'm a Jane. Those flyers are like kryptonite to me." I shoo away imaginary poison. "Can't go near them. Not standing in the same room as them."

Junie rolls her eyes.

"Check in with us tomorrow, Sherry," Lacey says. "We have lots to do if we're going to pull off a successful event by Saturday."

"And we gotta figure out how to keep it safe," I say. Lacey pales. She nods.

I sprint to the main entrance.

I'm barely at the curb, pinching my cheeks and biting my lips to get some color going, when Josh's mom pulls up.

Josh hops out so I can sit in the front. He is such a nice guy. He's cute, he's cool, he's polite and he's mine.

"Hi, Vicki," I say to Josh's mom. "Thanks for picking me up."

"No problem." She glances at my face. Her eyes widen, but she doesn't say anything about my lack of makeup. Vicki's cool that way. "Are you looking for something specific at Discount Mart?"

"Not really." I buckle up. "But I wouldn't mind checking out the video games."

"Did you hear about the most recent study comparing video games with the violence between Los Angeles gangs?" And she's off for the entire fifteen-minute car ride. The radio at the salon must be turned to the news all day every day, because Vicki's always up on current events and has loads of opinions.

Vicki leaves Josh and me at the outdoor café after telling us we have about an hour. Then she high-heel-clicks along the sidewalk, flashes her membership card and enters the store. She's a way cool mom.

Josh and I line up for huge slices of cheese pizza and all-you-can-drink soda. Once we're seated, our legs crossed under the table so that our feet are entwined, I tell him about Fantabulous You! and our planning meeting. "The trick is, we gotta make sure all the makeup is okay and safe. We're going to have to take turns keeping an eye on it."

"Count me in," Josh says.

Sigh. That's my guy.

"So"—a little frown crinkles his perfect-boyfriend forehead—"how are we gonna pull off this Discount Mart thing?"

I finish chewing. "I'm not exactly sure, but we need to see how Drew treats Lacey's packages. What if he believes her shipment is in jeopardy? That we're there to take it. How does he react?"

"And we're trying not to get in trouble, right?" Josh bites into his pizza.

"That would be good," I say, thinking of my good-behavior pact with the Academy. "Let's start with walking into shipping and receiving and finding Drew."

"And if he's there"—Josh sips his Dr Pepper— "we'll ask about the packages and I'll just pick them up and start walking out."

"Yeah, yeah, that's good. Be all bossy like you're taking over the packages and we'll see how protective he is."

Josh beams. He so likes to be involved and give good suggestions.

"If he's not there"—I poke the straw through the lid of my drink "we'll ask someone else about Lacey's stuff and then at least we can see where Drew's storing it." I push my paper plate with its half slice of pizza across the table.

"You sure you don't want it?" Josh asks.

"I'm saving room for samples," I say.

"Thanks."

Josh eats way more than me. Frighteningly more. I guess because of water polo and swim team.

When Josh's finished, we toss our trash. Then, hand in hand, we trek to the back of the store, visiting all the food sample tables on the way.

"This is cool, solving a mystery together." Josh pops a chicken dumpling in his mouth.

I nibble, nodding. I'm loving it too.

A bite of quiche and a tortilla chip + corn salsa later, and we're at the back of the store.

Josh points to an Employees Only sign. "This could be a problem."

"You're tall. You could easily pass for sixteen. Even sixteen and a half."

He strokes his chin where he'll probably grow a beard one of these days. "How about eighteen?"

"Yeah, maybe." Like my grandmother might think that. In dim light. If she'd forgotten her glasses were on top of her head instead of on her nose.

"You don't know this, Sherry, but I actually have

acting experience. Although it's way far back in my past."

"Really?"

"It was, like, in kindergarten, but I played a pretty good Oompa-Loompa. I even got to sing the Oompa-Loompa song."

Yowzer. My boyfriend was a child-star Oompa-Loompa! Because he's excellent at pretty much everything.

Josh drops down on one knee to tie his shoelace. When he's done, I fake pull him up. Then I give him a kiss for good luck. And then, because I have that kind of weak personality with a lack of willpower where I can't stop at only one M&M or only one rippled potato chip, I lean into Josh for another kiss.

"Hey, you two! What're you doing back here?"

Josh and I break apart.

Yikes! This is so not the kind of ruckus we planned to make. I sniff like a dog in a new neighborhood. Phew. No Cinnabon smell. Mrs. Howard would not consider getting caught kissing at the back of Discount Mart good behavior. I sniff again. Phew. No coffee smell. I'm not up for one of my mom's lectures about boys right now.

"What're you guys doin' back here?" says a blond guy in jeans and work boots and a tight Discount Mart T-shirt that shows off his rippling muscles. He's glaring at us with icy blue eyes. "This is a store, where families shop for diapers and vitamins and apple juice. This is not a make-out place." He steps closer. "How old're you two anyway? Twelve?"

"We are way past twelve." I gesture to Josh with my head. "He could pass for sixteen and a half." I sling my denim purse over my shoulder in anger. It's embarrassing enough to get caught kissing next to the bulk toilet paper in Discount Mart. No need to insult us about our age as well.

The guy pulls a walkie-talkie from his back pocket. "Do your parents know what you're doing back here?"

Ack. Eek. Ike. I do not want to be a store announcement. I peer at the name badge clipped to the pocket of his T-shirt. Drew!

Improv time. Although I was never an Oompa-Loompa. I stick out a hand. "Actually, Drew, we were looking for you."

He does not take my hand. "You were making out."

"Well, eventually, we would've been looking for you," I say.

"Lacey sent us," Josh says.

Oooh. From the way he jumps into character, Josh definitely has acting in his blood.

Drew steps back in confusion. He did not see that coming. "Lacey sent you?"

"Yeah, to pick up her makeup shipment," Josh says.

Drew crosses his arms. "No way."

"What do you mean, 'No way'?" I ask.

"That makeup is my responsibility. I keep it locked up with the cigarettes and alcohol." He yanks a cell phone from his front jeans pocket. It looks like a toy in his beefy hand. "I'm not handing anything over to anyone without Lacey's say-so."

"Oh, uh, it's okay." I'm stumbling over my words. I never envisioned the scenario playing out this far. "We won't take the makeup."

"Don't move." Drew pins us with his eyes, then presses the phone against his ear. "Lacey, a couple of kids are here asking for your packages." He listens, then says to us, "What're your names?"

"Just tell her it's Sherry," I say.

He repeats my name and listens some more. "She's here with a guy." He keeps on listening. Lacey is certainly chatting up a storm. "I got it. They're good kids. And, yeah, I can keep the packages." His voice goes all soft and mushy. "So, how are you?"

Josh checks a text on his phone. "We gotta go. My mom's waiting at the front of the store."

"Don't move," Drew says again.

I hope he's not planning to lock us up with the makeup.

Drew snaps his phone closed. He looks at us and starts nodding. And keeps on nodding, his eyes going all misty. "Thank you for helping her." He pounds his chest with his fist. "From here, guys." He pounds his chest again. "I'm thanking you from here."

I stick out my hand. This time, he grabs it, yanking me into a bear hug and patting me on the back. Except that with his strength, a pat knocks the air out of my lungs. "We gotta go, Drew," I gasp. "See ya around."

Josh reaches for Drew's hand. "Bye, man."

Drew grabs Josh up in a hug too, pummels his shoulder blades a few times, then releases him. "Thanks, man."

I make it home for dessert. The Ruler and I have this unspoken agreement where she breaks some of her nutzoid health-food rules and I break some of my sugary, fatty junk-food habits, and we meet somewhere close to the middle in the land called treats.

Tonight's dessert is brownies. The Ruler sticks with her aluminum-free baking powder and sea salt and rice flour. But, for me, she substitutes real chocolate chips for the bitter fake-o carob chips.

I slide into my chair at the kitchen table.

"How was dinner at Discount Mart?" The Ruler asks.

"Very pizza and soda." I pull the plate of brownies over to me. "And free samples."

"You missed my famous grilled burgers," my dad

says, "and, uh, delicious grilled teriyaki tofu." Of all of us, my dad's had the toughest time adjusting to The Ruler's healthy cooking. He's pretty much a red-meat addict. But he keeps trying, all in the name of love and lower cholesterol.

Family-ish chitchat ensues while I fork up bites of brownie. Sam and The Ruler have more gardening planned for the backyard. Dad bought a new CD by Céline Dion, his musical hero.

And then I'm up to my room. I text Junie to let her know Drew's not a makeup-business wrecker, just a very muscular lovesick puppy. So we're down to the Janes and Wacko Will as suspects.

I sprinkle fish flakes in the tank and gab with my bala sharks. I attack some math homework and put in time on my French-class presentation. Poor Kim will be *très, très* sorry she asked for separate grades. After the presentation, she'll probably beg to be my partner for the rest of the school year.

I'm eyeing my closet, picking out possible outfits for tomorrow. Outfits that will not point out my makeuplessness. So far, I have my jeans with bling + a hot pink T-shirt or plaid shorts + white T-shirt. I will make the final outfit decision tomorrow morning, depending on my mood.

There's a knock on my bedroom door.

The door cracks and Sam pokes in his head. "Sherry, I got something for you."

"Cool."

From his shorts pocket, he pulls out a small silver picture frame and hands it to me.

I stare at it.

It's a photo of me, Sam and Mom. It's the last photo of the three of us together.

"I bought the frame with the money I made selling plants and vegetables."

"Wow. Thanks." I swallow hard. "That was really nice of you, Sam." Little brothers. Who can figure them out? With Sam and me, the sister-brother relationship is probably a little less antagonistic than in other families. Because we lost our mother.

"Where are you going to put the picture?" he asks.

"I'll keep it with me for a while. Like in my backpack."

"That's what I thought you'd do." My brother looks me straight in the eye. "Do you ever kind of feel like Mom's still with us? Watching over us?"

My throat tightens. I nod. "Yeah."

"That's what I thought you'd say." Sam leaves.

I finish my homework. The house quiets down as everyone heads to bed. I'm half sitting, half lying on my bed, the light from the aquarium and the hum of the motor keeping me company. I go over the events of the past few days. There's the weird behavior of the Janes and their upcoming demonstration. And Wacko Will, who dances around the mall dressed as a chili pepper to encourage business. Plus Drew, who seems big and scary but is very kind to Lacey.

Chilling here all alone in the dim light of my room, I miss my mother. I miss joking around with her. I miss investigating with her. I miss discussing the case with her.

A feeling hard like a nut lodges in my stomach. I will solve this mystery. I will be perfectly behaved. Then, when I request five minutes of Real Time, Mrs. Howard will jump to say yes. And the foreign Academy will be so wowed by me that they'll invite me to sleuth for them with my mother. How will I get there? How will I convince The Ruler and my dad to let me go? I don't have to figure all that out today. First, I gotta solve the makeup mystery.

Tomorrow is Operation Break and Enter with Grandpa.

chapter
twenty-six

The school day passes in a fog. It's like when you have a fever, and you're in your own little world and slightly out of step with everyone else.

I'm in a mystery fog. All the pieces of the puzzle are bumping and shifting and crashing around in my brain, trying to fit together. It's brain tectonics.

I somehow navigate through my classes. All the way to French.

Even though Madame Blanchard is well aware that Kim and I are not actually working as partners for our *français* cultural project, she still forces us to sit next to each other in class. I am sort of waving a few of my more beautiful, flamboyant pages around. Kind of flaunting it to Kim that maybe she shouldn't have been so speedy to ask for separate grades. Her pages are all boring and typed and black and white.

It's practically the end of the period when Kim turns her head to speak with me.

"Look, Sherry, I probably shouldn't say anything." Kim zips and unzips her pencil case. "But you *are* dating my cousin and you *did* invite me to your slumber party. And I honestly don't think you're as mean as the rest of them think you are."

I have no idea what Kim is blathering on about.

"Tomorrow, at the Janes' meeting, they're"—she zips and unzips faster and faster—"going to kick you out."

"What?" I feel my face go slack with shock. In my entire life, I've never been kicked out of anything.

"You're just too, uh, radical for us. With all your violent ideas about sabotaging Naked Makeup cosmetics. We aren't interested in doing anything illegal like that."

"Oh." I lean back in my chair and tap my fingertips together. Well, that explains why I wasn't contacted by a Jane owning up to makeup tampering. I'm crossing the Janes off the suspect list. Which moves Will into first place. And I'm so busy mentally moving the mystery puzzle pieces around that I almost miss her next sentence.

"Besides kicking you out, they're planning to sort of, uh, embarrass you in front of everyone."

"What?"

From her backpack, she pulls out the plastic bag full of makeup I handed in at the last meeting. Then she pulls out my school cosmetics bag, the one a Jane confiscated from me a few mornings ago. She plunks the loot on my desk.

"The plan is to give you back your makeup."

"And that's supposed to embarrass me?" I'm hugging the bags to my chest, happy to have them home.

"Well, give it back, then force you to put some on in front of everybody." She stands. "You and the Janes? It just wasn't meant to be." Kim swings her heavy black backpack over her shoulder and trudges out of the classroom.

I slowly gather my stuff, bundling up my makeup bags and pushing them down into my denim purse. Yay for an oversized purse. I shove open the classroom door and step into the glaring Phoenix sun, shaking my head.

Embarrass me? They thought forcing me to put on makeup would embarrass me? More like it would be an educational lesson for the Janes. Kim's right. The Janes and I were so not meant to be.

I head over to the stone saguaro cactus in the middle of the courtyard, where Grandpa's perched on a thick arm, waiting for me. I suck in a couple of deep breaths, because honestly? Working with Grandpa is überstressful. He's a major loose cannon. I never

195

really know how he'll act. No one does. Also, he's difficult to understand. All in all, I've got legit worries that Operation Break and Enter might not go down smoothly.

It's up to Grandpa and me to get the scoop on Wacko Will and find out if he's next in line for a kiosk with a primo location. Josh, Nick, Amber and Lacey are out of commission for this part of the investigation because they can't know about Grandpa and his secret identity as a wren and the mascot for the Academy of Spirits. Junie could've helped but won't because there's a Latin club meeting after school. And she's the president.

As I edge up close to the statue, Grandpa squawks and flutters straight to my shoulder. I start sweating.

There are still oodles of students milling around and not one of them has a wren perched on her shoulder. I whisper out of the side of my mouth, "Grandpa, just fly along near me, but not like you're with me."

He squawks again, then zips up in the air, circling overhead.

Grandpa and I trundle along. A car honks, then another, the drivers pointing up to Grandpa, who's keeping a distance of a couple of feet above me, but I guess it's obvious we're together.

I do not want this kind of attention. This is not the kind of write-up I want on the ghost Internet.

Mrs. Howard would so not be impressed with me or Grundpa.

The sec there's a lull in traffic, I say, "Grandpa, people are noticing us. In a 'that girl looks like a total weirdo' sort of way." My arm up high, I wave him forward. "Meet me at the mall entrance."

He rasps out a string of unintelligible syllables and zips off.

By the time I get to the mall, Grandpa's already perched patiently in the big metal O of "Phoenix" in the Phoenix Mall sign above the entrance. I wave a Ziploc bag of sunflower seeds in his direction, then drop it in my denim purse. I hold the purse wide open.

He beelines for the opening and dives in, burying his head in the seeds. His ragged tail feathers poke up.

I gently push his bottom down and lightly hold the purse closed. So far, so good. He's contained, and I can sneak him into the mall.

I pull my phone from my jeans pocket, place it on my shoulder, then lean my ear against it. This way, I can talk with Grandpa, let him know the plan, and I'll just look like a million other people, chatting on a cell in public.

"Grandpa, ya gotta stay in my purse. You can't go flying around the mall, and you definitely cannot zip over to the food court for a big munch session. Once we get to the mall manager's office, I'll let you out so you can check the files." I fill in a bunch more details about what he's looking for and how we'll handle it if the manager's actually in the office.

Grandpa pokes out his little birdy head and says, "Okay."

All in all, I'm feeling more confident with each step. I march past Brittani's Baubles and Movie World and Sequins.

March. March. March. This can definitely work. I'm all focused on A, then B, then C, totally lost in my detective plan.

"Sherry!" My little brother barrels into me. Going about one hundred miles per hour.

I'm careening, losing balance, falling. I grab for a bench. Fingers grasping, clasping around a wooden slat. In the process, my big, heavy, overpacked purse slips off my shoulder, over my elbow, past my wrist.

It lands with a thump under the bench.

A balding cactus wren hops out, shakes his feathers and blinks his beady black eyes.

chapter
twenty-seven

Sam blinks back at Grandpa. "Is that John Wayne?" Sam blinks at me. "John Wayne was in your purse?"

I lean over to grab my bag and whisper out of the side of my mouth to Grandpa, "Meet me at the office."

With a raspy, "Okay," Grandpa flaps off, flying high up by the vaulted ceiling. A mother points him out to her toddler, but for the most part, shoppers are looking at window displays or buying merchandise or talking with their friends. No one really notices him.

I stand, narrow my eyes at Sam and catapult into my annoyed-big-sister routine. "Don't act like you don't know what's going on, Sam. I am so not falling for it this time. I don't know how you got a bird into my purse. I don't even want to know why you put a bird in my purse. But did you even stop to think for one tiny second what a bird might do in my purse? Think of the windshield of a car. I do not even want to check to see. I should probably just go directly to a trash can and throw out this purse. Which was not cheap." I continue to rant and rave until his eight-year-old eyes glaze over.

When I finally stop, he says in a small voice, "Sherry, I didn't do it."

"John Wayne just happened to fly into my purse? I'm being bird-stalked?" I say, all incredulous. "That *is* creepy."

"At least he's a nice bird," Sam says. "He never pecks Grandma or anything. And he did seem to like you the other day."

"I do not want to be bird-stalked. Ewww." I stick out my tongue.

"We don't even know where he is now. Do you think he'll be okay?" Sam asks. "He's Grandma's favorite bird."

"Yeah." I roll my eyes like there's no doubt. "He'll eat dinner at the food court, then fly back to Grandma's." I hike up my purse on my shoulder. "Anyway, what are you doing here?"

"Paula decided I needed new clothes." He pulls on

the hem of his shorts, which are definitely riding nerdishly high.

"Where is she?" I'm swiveling my head, looking around.

"Restroom." He turns to retrace his steps. "But I'm supposed to wait at that bench for her." He points.

"Okay. And remind her that I'm here to help plan the Naked Makeup thing."

He nods and races off.

I head in the opposite direction and hang a left at the Mug Shoppe. Then I stride down an empty hallway. I pass a baby-changing room. The next door is the mall office.

One thing I can say about Grandpa is that he has an excellent sense of direction. Also, although I have trouble understanding him, he always understands me. So I'm pretty sure he'll be at the mall office. But my stomach won't unclench until I see the white of his patchy skin.

I'm practically at the end of the hallway before I spot him above a door. An orange Cheeto dangles from his beak.

He squawks when he sees me and the Cheeto falls to the floor.

I put up a hand like a stop sign, as in, *Don't fly to me. Let me sneakily check out the office to see if the mall manager is in there.*

I poke my head around the corner. A bearded man

with glasses and a bald head like an egg is tap-tapping on a keyboard, engrossed in whatever numbers are flashing up on the computer screen.

I quickly back up, out of his sight. Then I dig in my purse for a package of gum. I'm very grateful Grandpa behaved himself and didn't leave me any surprises. My fingers finally close on some sugarless peppermint. I pop out a couple of pieces and toss them in my mouth. Then I chomp like a fiend.

I hide the chewed-up gum inside my fist before waltzing into the office. "Hi! I'm doing a school project on the number of teens hired by malls and which stores they work in and how long they work for and if they usually quit or are fired and what they're fired for and how much they make and how often they get raises." I could go on forever. Rambling is one of my specialties.

But the man's shaking his head so fast, he's blurry. "That's a lot of information you're asking for. Most of which I don't have. You could try going from store to store, but some of those details are confidential." He's still shaking his head as he turns his attention back to the computer. "What are today's teachers thinking?"

"They are so crazy." My eyes are on him while my fingers press my still-warm-and-pliable gum into the doorjamb. "Total waste of our tax money."

Back in the hallway, I give a quick thumbs-up to Grandpa, then duck into the diaper-changing room, where I pull out my cell, scroll down through Contacts to where I've stored the phone number for this office and press Send.

"Grant Peabody, Phoenix Mall."

In a high-pitched English accent, I say, "This is Victoria from the British Import store. Our rep, Julia Simon, from the London head office—London, England, that is—is visiting and has some questions about mall advertising that only you can answer." The British Import store is the farthest from the mall office.

"That's fine," Mr. Peabody says, "I'm in the office. Just send her this way."

Ack. I lower my voice, like I don't want Julia Simon to hear. "I don't think that's a good idea. Ms. Simon has asked if you could come to us. She's talking about dropping extra advertising money on our location, so . . ."

"Extra advertising money?" I hear Mr. Peabody's chair scrape across the floor. "I'll be right over."

I count to ten, then exit the diaper-changing area just as a mom and a screaming smelly baby enter.

His back to me, Mr. Peabody's rounding the corner into the main part of the mall. He's clipping a neon yellow walkie-talkie to his belt.

I hip-push open the office door, which never locked, thanks to my coolio gum-in-the-doorjamb trick.

Grandpa swoops in.

203

I stand guard at the threshold. I so do not want to get caught breaking and entering. If Grandpa gets busted, they'll shoo him out of the mall. If I get busted, I'll have to listen to parental lectures until my hair grows gray and I start wearing socks with sandals.

Grandpa flutters in front of the gunmetal gray file cabinet, then braces his little legs against the second drawer. He huffs. He puffs. He coughs.

The drawer slowly cracks open. His yellow beak on the handle and his wings working overtime, Grandpa pulls.

Oh, fine. I can't take the tension anymore. I nip into the office and tug open the file drawer. I scoot back to my lawful position.

Grandpa balances on the files, his claws gripping tight and his beak poking and prodding through papers. He's mumbling a bunch of gibberish, probably the names of the files.

Suddenly, he squawks a happy squawk, then tugs on a file. His whole little body strained, he tugs and tugs. Finally, a manila file folder swinging from his beak, he starts to lift off.

Whoosh. The file drifts to the floor, papers coasting through the air and then gliding along the linoleum.

Crackle. Crackle. The static of a walkie-talkie breaks the silence!

"I'll pick it up from my office and take it straight to the south entrance. Over." It's Mr. Peabody!

Footsteps!

Footsteps getting louder!

He's headed this way!

Ack! Eek! Ike!

chapter
twenty-eight

"Grandpa!" I whisper urgently. "He's back!"

Grandpa looks up from the floor, where he's hopping from paper to paper, scooting them into a pile.

An open file drawer. Papers spilled all over the floor. A cactus wren.

Yikes!

There's no time to unstick the gum from the doorjamb. I yank the door shut, then raise my fist and knock.

Mr. Peabody arrives and spots me. He frowns. "Roger. Over and out." He clips the walkie-talkie back on his belt loop, still frowning.

He pulls a key ring from his pocket. "Is there something else?" he asks me, in that tone adults use when they're busy and you're interrupting and they just want you to disappear. Of course, he did just hike the whole way across the mall to speak to a nonexistent British person named Julia.

Mr. Peabody's fumbling through the keys.

"Uh, do you know how many pounds of potatoes are used each day at the American Potato Company?"

"I have no idea. What kind of question is that? What's the name of your school?" He bites off the words with impatience.

"Donner Middle School." I name a rival school.

"What are you doing all the way over here?

"I love this mall. Everyone is so friendly. Like yourself."

He holds up a key and inserts it in the lock.

Blood roars in my ears.

He turns the key.

I close my eyes.

Silence. Nothing from Mr. Peabody. Nothing from Grandpa.

I open my eyes.

No papers. No Grandpa. No open file drawer.

I practically crumple to the ground in relief. Instead, I charge into the diaper-changing room. It's empty. But smelly. With the door cracked, I listen for Mr. Peabody to leave.

The second he hustles down the hall, I'm back at

the office door. Which still opens because of the gum. "Grandpa," I whisper.

He backs out from under the desk, dragging the file folder behind him.

I step into the room and pick up the folder. I open my purse and Grandpa flies in. I peel the gum from the lock, then shut the door.

And we explode outta there.

I rocket all the way to the main entrance, where I open my purse and Grandpa skips to the ground.

"Thanks, Grandpa. I owe you."

He shakes his head and shrugs his feathery shoulders. "We're family."

"How'd you ever get everything cleaned up so fast?" I ask. "I was sweating bullets."

I don't understand a syllable of his reply.

"Tell Mom hi."

"Sure," he says, zooming straight up and away.

I plop down on a bench and open the file. It has a blue sticky label: KIOSKS.

Way to go, Grandpa!

The papers in the file are all wild and crazy out of order. I just start flipping through them. And stop when I hit pay dirt.

Contacts Form: William Barley.
May 5: William Barley signs

six-month contract for Kiosk #17.

May 7: Complaint from WB that kiosks are not secure enough at night. Presence of mall security at night does not calm him down.

May 9: Complaint from WB about kiosk storage space.

May 10: WB complains because two stores across from his kiosk are going out of business. He feels this will negatively impact his kiosk sales.

May 11: Complaint from WB that not enough foot traffic goes by his kiosk. He is actively counting foot traffic at other kiosk locations.

May 12: Based on his observations, WB wants a kiosk closer to the food court, specifically the location currently occupied by Naked Makeup.

May 13: WB insistent on know-

ing how quickly he can procure
food-court kiosk location.

Wow. Wacko Will seriously wants Lacey's kiosk! As
in seriously. And what a pain-in-the-neck kiosk
renter. He started grumbling right from the start and
he gripes more and more frequently as time goes on.
I thumb through a bunch more papers.

Until my fingers land on it—a sheet with a title
in big fat uppercase letters. KIOSK LOCATIONS:
WAITING LIST.

Will's in the first position!

Which means Will is poised to take over the next
available kiosk. Which gives him a very strong motive for forcing Lacey out of hers. Forcing her out by
tainting her makeup with extra papaya acid, hot pepper juice and cactus spines.

Wacko Will Barley, I am so on to you!

I shove the papers back in the file folder. I'll show
Junie, Amber and Lacey the evidence. Then, when
the coast is clear, I'll scoot the file under the office
door. Grandpa and I can't risk breaking in again.
Mr. Peabody will always wonder how his file folder
hopped out of the cabinet and came to relax on the
floor of his office.

My phone vibrates. I tuck the file under my arm
and check the text. It's Junie. She's walking into the

mall. I text back to let her know I'm headed to Naked Makeup.

We arrive from opposite directions. I'm only a few seconds ahead of her.

The kiosk is a hubbub of activity.

I stand back for a minute and just watch.

An iPod hooked up to cute little speakers blasts out a catchy upbeat tune.

Hips swinging in time to the music, Lacey's placing teal flyers along the counter. Amber twirls in, shoulders shaking, and presses perfume-scented sticker samples on the bottom of each page.

They're laughing and dancing and singing and smacking hands when they pass close to each other. Even in high heels they don't miss a step. There isn't a customer in sight, but Amber and Lacey don't look worried. They look happy and busy. Because they have a plan.

Lacey waves to us. "Sherry! Junie! You're part of this. Come on." We start singing along and moving closer to Amber and Lacey. We all bump hips. Amber even smiles at us.

We start planning Fantabulous You! Lacey has a binder with dividers and lined notepaper where she's jotting down all the details.

I'm reading the list of products she wants to use for the classes, when someone covers my eyes. It's

Josh! He's here with Nick, both of them ready to talk security.

I open the file and pull out the two incriminating papers. Everyone is really impressed with my gum-in-the-lock trick and my Victoria-the-British-store-keeper phone call. I even demo my English accent for them. Of course, I leave out Grandpa's part in the story. Only Junie knows he was with me.

"Unfortunately, it's only circumstantial evidence," I say.

"I don't get it," Lacey says.

"Meaning it's not *actual* proof," Nick says.

"We're just assuming it's Will because we're putting two and two together," Junie says, "and coming up with four."

"We need hard proof," I say. "And I've got an idea for how to get it. It involves Josh and Nick and tricking Will on *Revealing Phoenix*."

"I think I know where you're going, Sherry," Nick says, his eyes all squinty and concentrating. "While we're taping, we accidentally-on-purpose let slip some information about where a new shipment of makeup is or something like that. Then we lie in wait to tape when he goes to tamper with it."

My jaw drops. Never in a million bajillion years did I think Nick and I would be on the exact same wavelength.

"Tricking Will sounds like a great plan." The frown

is back across Lacey's forehead. "But how're we gonna fit that in before Fantabulous You!?"

"We can't," Junie says. "Which means he'll be on the loose and looking to do damage at the event."

We move into a discussion about security and safeguarding the makeup products and keeping Will away from the kiosk.

"Nick and I can tail him on Saturday," Josh says. "Constantly."

"Sprinkle baby powder all over the kiosk at closing each evening," I suggest. "Then it's easy to see if anything's been touched."

"We've already had a huge response to our Fantabulous You! classes." Lacey's voice is shaky. "Any makeup mishaps, and it's the end of my business."

"But if everything goes right, Naked Makeup will totally take off," Amber says, her eyes sparkling. "You guys should tape Fantabulous You!"

"Sherry and I could take over Will detail when Nick and Josh start taping," Junie says.

I nod slowly. This is getting complicated.

"To really do it right," Nick says, "we'll need two cameras. I know a guy who'll lend us one."

Nick and Josh take off to borrow another camera.

Lacey's cell rings. Another client for a Fantabulous You! morning slot.

The picture of a certain someone and her long gray braid pops into my mind. "Can I reserve a spot for my grandmother?" I ask. "She's finally ready to update her makeup and hair. Well, to start wearing makeup."

"Absolutely." Lacey writes down *Sherry's grandmother.* "Consider her in."

Amber sends Junie and me out to the parking lot to slip flyers under the wipers of each car.

I stop distributing flyers when Brianna calls.

"Sherry, big news!" Brianna says.

"Your parents broke down and are giving you a clothing allowance?" I say.

"Well, not quite that big." Brianna pauses. "I quit the Janes."

"Smart girl!"

"Actually, they asked me to leave. I'm fine with it, though. I was starting to cheat a little with my mascara wand. And, uh, my new palette of eye shadow. And a very, very light application of rose lip gloss."

"It was a strange club, Bri. Even the Latin club would be better." Then I tell Brianna all about Fantabulous You!

"I'll call for an afternoon appointment," Brianna says, all excited. "I can't go in the morning because I'm getting my hair cut up to my chin."

"Seriously?"

"Yeah, I'm tired of being an oblong. I want to live life as an oval."

"I don't think a haircut will actually change the

214

shape of your face," I say slowly. "But it can minimize your oblongness."

"Don't wreck this for me, Sherry."

I can see what she's saying. Because Brianna's had a tough few days, with learning the truth about her face shape, suffering through ravaged skin and joining the Janes. She so deserves a break.

"I'm calling Lacey right now for an appointment." She disconnects.

I go back to passing out flyers. And I'm mid-wiper when it suddenly hits me.

There's one other person I need to consult.

chapter
twenty-nine

I arrive home to an empty house. There's a note from my dad propped up against the sea salt and pepper on the counter.

Sam is at baseball practice. Paula and I will bring him home. Love, Dad

I do what any self-respecting thirteen-year-old detective with a ghost mother and a bunch of worries would do. Grab some coffee beans and barrel out to the pear tree in the backyard.

I've barely got the espresso beans in the air when there's a whiff of coffee, a big tremble of the tree and a thud. My mother has landed. I think she's missed me as much as I've missed her.

The branch where I'm sitting shakes as she settles

in. It keeps right on shaking, but gently. I'm guessing she's jiggling her leg, a habit she's had for as long as I can remember.

"Mom, I have to admit something." I'm nervous, twirling my hair around my index finger.

"Okay," she says slowly.

And I spill. All about how I'm still investigating the makeup mystery. Even though Mrs. Howard told me to stop. And how my goal is to wow the Academy and every single spirit who surfs the WWWD so that the foreign Academy that's considering my mother will also consider me. And how I want five minutes of Real Time. Then I fill her in on all the details of the mystery.

When I'm finally done, I take a deep breath. And wait.

My mom clears her throat. "That would be great if we were teamed up for the foreign Academy. Logistically, it would be tricky to work out. With you in school and me a secret. But it would truly be amazing." The branch bobs as she shifts. "Your work on the makeup mystery is impressive. I'm proud of you."

"Why don't *I* feel better about it, then? Instead of like I'm about to take a huge important test at school and I never studied." A shiver snakes up my spine. "I keep going over all the details for Saturday. It seems as though we have all our bases covered, but I have a bad feeling."

"Listen to that feeling." Mom's voice is serious. "You're honing your detective's intuition. Remember we were at Pat and Oscar's restaurant the night I died?"

I nod. Even when I'm wrinkled and gray and my false teeth are clicking away in my mouth, I will recall the details of that night.

"Sitting there with you, Sam and Dad, a migraine hammering my head, I had the kind of bad feeling you're describing. I ignored it. Granted, I didn't realize things were going to turn deadly. But let's just say I'm a huge believer in detective intuition now."

Ack! Eek! Ike!

I freeze. Even my lungs are frozen solid and I can't get a breath in or out.

"Sherry, I'm not trying to scare you. I don't for a second think the makeup mystery is a life-or-death situation. Just be grateful you have that bad feeling, and trust it. Which means you should be extra careful, extra vigilant, extra on-guard for the event."

"Thanks, Mom." And I can breathe again.

"Sherry, would you feel better if I hung around the mall for a while on Saturday?"

"Seriously? Even though Mrs. Howard said you couldn't help?"

"I'll be there for moral support," Mom says slowly. "That shouldn't cause a problem with the Academy."

"How's everything going for you?"

"Great. I'm really pushing myself skillwise with the animals. Although it's hard constantly being observed."

My phone rings.

"See you tomorrow." My mom flies really close to me. "I miss you, pumpkin." She takes off.

I flip open my phone. "Hi, Josh!"

"Whatcha doin?"

Sitting in a pear tree, chatting with my ghost mother. "Just thinking over Saturday."

"It's a rockin' plan. Nick and I can totally tag-team Will. My mom gave me money to buy some of his hot sauce. I'll take my time choosing."

It's so adorable how he's getting into the investigation.

I hope he's right about the plan rockin'.

I hope nothing goes wrong.

chapter
thirty

On Saturday morning, the sun rises early and starts doing its thing. It's already toasty by the time I'm traipsing over to the mall.

I arrive just as security is unlocking the doors for the day. A knot of worry coils in my stomach.

When I get to the Naked Makeup kiosk, I suck in a breath. The kiosk is totally transformed and über-beautiful.

On top, there's a wide shiny pink and lavender banner announcing FANTABULOUS YOU! Plus there are matching balloons. Each side of the booth has two chairs, making four stations. Amber will man one side while Lacey handles the other. Speaking of which, they're nowhere to be seen.

And the stations? Übercute in shades of pink and lavender. Draped over the chair backs are smocks for the customers. A few items, like palettes of eye shadow and pots of blush and different brushes, are lined up perfectly. Metallic confetti in butterfly shapes is sprinkled along the kiosk counter. Each station is equipped with a long-handled round mirror lying facedown, ready to show a client her stunning post-appointment self.

I have an incoming text from Josh.

<nick & i r in place. our phones fully charged. will in chili pepper outfit & opening kiosk now>

As I'm texting back <gr8!>, a text from Junie comes through.

<running late. ETA 15 min>

I drop my phone in my purse. I sniff for coffee. No Mom yet. I'll worry less with her here. Maybe.

"What do ya think?" Lacey's walking toward me, carrying a case of mini water bottles. Amber's on her heels with a large purple plastic bucket.

"Amazing." I give a thumbs-up.

She beams, then drops the case by the end of the kiosk.

Amber places the bucket next to the case and disappears to the other side of the kiosk while Lacey starts transferring water bottles into the bucket.

"Anything show up with the baby powder?" I ask as

I pick up a couple of bottles and drop them in the bucket.

"Thanks," Lacey says. "Nothing. The powder was totally untouched. I just brought in the Hair Repair Extraordinaire from my trunk. Amber's unpacking it now and mixing in some basic flower scents."

"Why don't you let Sherry handle the water?" Amber peeks around from her side of the kiosk. "You can do the giveaway samples."

While I'm loading up the water, I glance at Amber and Lacey. In matching lavender capris, fitted pink T-shirts and heels, they're as beautiful as the kiosk. The whole place reeks of sophistication.

Shoppers begin drifting by. They slow down to stare at the kiosk. A few ask questions and sign up for the remaining makeup appointments later in the day. The morning sessions are booked solid. A circle of people, mostly girls and women, mill around the kiosk. They're browsing and chatting, waiting for the show to begin.

I keep an eye out for Grandma and Junie. I keep a nose out for Mom.

Lacey pushes a stray strand of hair behind an ear and says to me, "We can pull this off without a crisis, right?"

"We're good," I say, but the worry coils tighter.

"Sherry!" Grandma clomps toward me, her frizzy

gray braid swinging from side to side. Her face is completely au naturel, her eyelashes short and stubby, her eyebrows uneven, her skin drab. She needs a makeover more than most people on the planet. Probably she won't recognize her transformed self in the mirror.

Lacey shows Grandma where she'll be sitting. "I'll be your cosmetician," Lacey says.

"Glad to meet you." Grandma squeezes my shoulder. "Sherry talked me into this, and I have to say I haven't been this excited about trying something new since I switched to Egg Beaters."

"You'll love the results." Her head to the side, Lacey's assessing Grandma's face. "We have the perfect foundation for you."

"Well, this old body is ready for some changes." Grandma narrows her eyes at Lacey. "And you're sure your products aren't tested on animals? Especially not on birds?" Grandma frowns, like she's imagining someone infiltrating her backyard to coat mascara on her precious birds' feathers.

"Definitely no testing on animals." Lacey straightens already straight product on the shelf. "I've never heard of anyone testing on birds, but Naked Makeup doesn't test on any animals. Period." Lacey smiles her confident, megawatt smile. "You're safe with us."

"I'm counting on it." Grandma clunks to the counter. She hunches over bottles of product, holding them close to her face to read the small print.

Where are Junie and my mother?

Crystal arrives with a pair of drinks from Jazzed-Up Juice. She pulls straws from her shirt pocket. "Amber, Lacey, I had them squirt in an extra ounce of energy supplement. You'll need it with the busy day you have ahead." She strides back to where Amber's screwing lids on bottles of foundation and pitches in.

My cell pings with a text from Josh.

<suspect heading your way. we r following him but need to set up our equipment. can u take ovr surveillance?>

<yes> My pulse quickens. I step away from the booth and see a tall chili pepper prancing toward me. Josh and Nick trail behind him.

You'd think keeping track of a dancing chili pepper would be easy. But nooo. Will is in constant motion. He dashes and darts among the meandering shoppers, slowing to moonwalk by the Hallmark store's window display, then picking up speed again with a salsa move. Next he crouches down to retrieve something from the floor.

The next thing I know, I'm squinting and shading my eyes. I can't see him anywhere!

I leave my post by the giveaways and the water and

jog down the aisle. Maybe he cut into the Hallmark store? Negative. The food court? Negative. The restroom? Can't check there.

I'm a few feet from the kiosk when I spot the familiar pepper costume. I jet over. Will's hopping from one foot to the other, opening bottles and sniffing.

Totally engrossed with customers, Amber and Lacey are oblivious!

"Will! What? What? What?" I sputter. "What are you doing?" I grab the bottle he has up to his nose. "You can't just go around opening stuff," I say in a loud voice, like I've got some authority. Not that it's ever easy to be thirteen and pull that off.

Where are Junie and my mom?

"What's going on?" Crystal pops up from where she was crouched under the counter by an open cupboard. Both her hands are filled with mini mascaras. With her heel, she closes the cupboard door.

"He's opening bottles." I work hard at not shrieking. What's with all these people hanging back here on a day when we're trying to keep the makeup safe?

"I was just sniffing. Who buys without sniffing first?" Will points to the banner on the roof. "What's going on anyway?"

Crystal spills the mascaras into a small wicker basket. "Lacey wanted more giveaways," she says to me.

She grasps Will's elbow. "It's an all-day cosmetics extravaganza. Lacey and Amber are providing make-overs." She steers him toward the crowd. "You should stay and watch." She glances over her shoulder and gives me a thumbs-up.

"Hi, Sherry!" Josh calls from the side of the kiosk with Lacey's stations. Next to him, Nick is hunkered down over a zippered camera bag.

I wave.

Will wrestles his elbow free from Crystal and stomps over to the guys. "You're taping them too?" he says, his voice raised in annoyance.

Josh doesn't flinch or look up from where he's kneeling, fiddling with a tripod. He's so cool, even under pressure. Maybe from all those tense water polo games with close scores. Or maybe he was just born cool.

"Yeah, dude," Josh says. "Remember we told you how the mall manager wants us to interview all kinds of mall personnel so he can run different tapes at the information desk?" Josh twists the tripod legs tight.

"It's in your best interest for us to garner a decent-sized audience." Nick's pulling cables from the camera bag.

Why does Nick always sound like he swallowed a dictionary?

"Sherry!" Junie's running toward us, her red hair streaming out like a tail.

Suddenly, the smell of coffee gusts next to me. My mom!

"Sorry I'm late, Sherry. Academy stuff. Everything under control here?"

"I think so," I whisper. If under control is a knot threatening to twist up my entire insides.

"How much longer do you guys need?" Lacey says from the center of a circle of customers.

"Five minutes max." Nick's screwing a camera into the tripod. "We got that extra camera, so we can record on both sides of the kiosk and get you and Amber doing makeovers at the same time. And we got the cordless mic set up like you wanted."

"You guys rock," Lacey says.

Amber makes her way over to Lacey and hands her a spray bottle of Hair Repair Extraordinaire. "I ended up going with gardenia."

Junie skids up next to me, panting. "Sorry." *Pant.* "My mom." *Pant.* "Chores."

"Sherry, Junie," Lacey says, "could you grab the Naked Makeup business cards and giveaways and start distributing them?"

"Where's your grandmother, Sherry?" Amber asks. "She wandered off."

What? She'll miss her appointment. And keep her sad gray braid for another two or three decades.

I glance at Will. He's still next to Josh, hands on his hips. Well, if chili peppers have hips.

"Watch Will," I say quietly to Junie. "And just so you know, my mom's here."

Wiping sweat off her shiny forehead, Junie says, "No prob. I can keep an eye on him while I'm handing out stuff. You go find your grandmother."

"I'm on it too," Mom says to me.

I nod thanks to both of them, then take off for the closest dorky store. Birkenstock Shoes.

I've barely rounded the corner when I spot Grandma at the front of the store near the display window. She's bent over, trying on clunky, square clogs. "Come on, Grandma." I grab her hand. "It's time for your makeover. Maybe we can go shoe shopping together later."

"That would be lovely, Sherry." Grandma slips off a pair of lame new shoes and slips on her lame used ones.

"Heels would really slenderize your ankles," I remark.

Grandma shoots me a sharp look.

At the kiosk, Lacey's talking into the microphone, giving a brief history of makeup and Naked Makeup to an ever-growing crowd of shoppers. Crystal's hanging at the back of everyone, out of the way. Doing that twisty thing with her earring. Will's sitting cross-legged in the front of the audience.

Mr. Peabody's here too. Like a squirrel's, his eyes are bright and alert and flitting around. He's taking in the number of interested customers. A small smile plays on his lips. When his eyes pass over me, he doesn't even wave hello.

The three other makeover clients are already seated.

I guide Grandma in the direction of the empty seat on Lacey's side. Then I swoop up a handful of business cards and a basket of freebies and start circulating through the crowd.

There's an odd, mildly irritating smell that I can't identify. Maybe someone's cooking a new dish in the food court?

"The first thing you'll notice about Naked Makeup is the superiority of the product." While talking, Lacey unbraids Grandma's hair. "You'll love wearing it. Love the way it makes you look. And love the way it feels." She waves the spray bottle. "Hair Repair Extraordinaire. We call this our hair miracle in a bottle." She uncaps it. "Goodbye, frizz!"

Lacey sprays it liberally on the top of Grandma's hair. Then she lifts up chunks and sprays under them. And then she sprays around Grandma's ears. "Hello, manageable hair!" Lacey sprays the limp, shoulder-length dark hair of the twentysomething girl seated next to Grandma. "Hello, shine!"

Amber steps close to Lacey, her hands out, ready for the miracle spray and the microphone.

By now I'm finished giving out the freebies. I position myself at the side of the crowd, where I have a good view. Will's still at the front, the only person sitting on the floor.

Junie's across from me. Our eyes meet, and she gives me a thumbs-up.

Mom breezes in next to me. "Everything looks secure."

The crowd is quiet, expectant. Mr. Peabody's eyes jump from Lacey to Amber to the crowd to the beauty clients to Josh and Nick. He's nodding to himself, looking pleased.

It's all dramatic and well timed. They're so professional, Amber and Lacey could be a Las Vegas act.

"Goodbye, frizz!" With arcing arm movements, Amber sprays the first client on her side, a mother with short, curly mousy hair. "Hello, management and shine!" Amber moves to the fourth client, a teen with long, straight blond hair.

"Why is Hair Repair Extraordinaire the best hair product on the market? Because it works. It works on dry hair. Or on wet hair." Amber zips to the end of the kiosk, where she and Lacey meet up like a choreographed dance act. "And it works fast for those mornings when you're getting ready for work or for school."

"So fast that our first client is ready to be brushed out," Lacey says into the mic Amber's holding.

The two cosmeticians sashay to Grandma. Lacey picks up a large vent brush.

Suddenly, I sniff a faint sugar + cinnamon smell.

Mrs. Howard!

The scent's getting stronger. She's getting closer. She's here to spy on me. And she'll spot Mom! Right in the middle of the mystery I'm not supposed to be solving.

"Mom!" I whisper, panic bubbling up my throat. "It's Mrs. Howard! You gotta leave. Now."

"Too late, Sherry," Mom says. "She sees me."

Within milliseconds, the Cinnabon smell lands full force behind me. Mrs. Howard remains silent. Spying like a big sneaky ghost.

I turn my attention back to the beauty show and ignore her.

"First, you brush the product through the hair evenly," Amber comments.

Lacey places the bristles on Grandma's crown.

Grandma clamps her eyes shut.

The brush on an angle, Lacey pulls downward.

A clump of Grandma's frizzy gray hair hits the ground.

chapter
thirty-one

I t all happens in painful slow motion.

At first, there's utter and complete silence. Like that expression about hearing a pin drop.

Then a gasp ripples through the crowd.

Amber and Lacey have turned to stone, like the White Witch from Narnia just sledded by and zapped them with her evil wand.

Mouth totally agape, the twentysomething girl next to Grandma lifts a hand to her scalp. A hunk of dark hair comes away in her fist. She screams.

Grandma opens her eyes. She looks at the girl with a handful of hair and a bald patch on the side of her head. Grandma's eyes dart to the floor where the clump of her gray hair lies like a dead animal.

She combs her fingers through her bangs. Strands come loose. She screams.

From the other side of the kiosk, Amber's two clients race over. Their eyes widen like Frisbees. They put their hands to their heads and pull out tufts. They scream.

Finally, the mall manager comes to life. "Move along, people." With big arm movements, he shoos the crowd away. "The situation is under control."

Which it totally is not. Four screaming women. Two frozen cosmeticians. Two guys taping. Clumps of hair dotting the ground.

One mother ghost caught at the scene of the crime. One spying guidance-counselor ghost.

And me. A girl who signed her grandmother up for this event. A grandmother who wore her braid for decades. Poor Grandma.

Twinkle gone from his eyes and smile gone from his lips, Mr. Peabody says all serious and military to Amber and Lacey, "Give me the spray."

Amber hands it over in a jerky strobelike motion.

"Lock up the kiosk."

In a daze, Lacey follows his orders.

A security guy strides up to Mr. Peabody.

"Don't leave this kiosk. Don't let anyone near it," Mr. Peabody says. Without even looking at Amber and Lacey, he points his arm. "You two. My office. Now."

Josh and Nick are catching it all on tape.

Will is handing out coupons for his hot sauces.

Like zombies, Amber and Lacey do what they're told. They're ashen, almost translucent.

Junie moves next to me. "What's he going to do with them?"

"He'll release Amber to her parents because she's a minor," my mother says to me. "He'll hand Lacey over to the police."

Yikes. I pass the info on to Junie.

The smell of burnt sugar is nauseating.

"Christine," Mrs. Howard says with low and controlled fury. "Look on top of the kiosk."

I hear my mother suck in a breath. "The foreign Academy! How long has their agent been here?"

I sniff. So that strange smell isn't from the food court. It's the foreign Academy spy.

"He witnessed it all," Mrs. Howard says. "Sherry, you have ruined everything."

chapter
thirty-two

Josh, Junie, Nick and I are in the food court.

All around us, people are buzzing about the incident at Fantabulous You!

Mrs. Howard's words swim in my head. *Sherry, you have ruined everything.* I have to talk to my mother.

I couldn't face food right now if you paid me, but Josh and Nick are scarfing down roast beef sandwiches. What is it with guys?

"I don't get it," Josh says. "When did Will get a chance to mess with the hair spray?"

I'm wondering the same thing. Amber and Lacey checked out all the product last night. The baby powder was undisturbed. Lacey didn't even unpack the hair spritz until this morning. Josh and Nick stuck to

Will like Krazy Glue. Junie and I were on him once he got to the kiosk.

"It wasn't Will," I say. "That's the only explanation that makes sense."

"That's logical," Nick says. This is a big compliment from him.

"And I bet the culprit was there, in the crowd, watching," I say. "Bad guys often return to watch their handiwork."

"Let's look at the tapes," Junie says.

Nick's already unzipping the camera bag closest to him.

The smell of coffee wafts by me. My mother!

I excuse myself, race to the restroom and lock myself in a stall. Anyone hearing me talk will assume I'm on my cell.

"I went to the office," my mother says.

"How are Amber and Lacey?" I ask.

"Amber left with her parents." She pauses. "Lacey's pretty upset. The police used words like 'assault' and 'aggravated assault.' That really scared her. They're escorting her down to the station for more questioning."

"Poor Lacey."

"The best thing we can do for her is to catch the real perp," my mom says.

"Any idea what was in the product to make the hair fall out?"

"Hair-B-Gone," she says. "It's a hair-removal spray or cream you get at the drugstore. It comes in a yellow bottle. You apply it to your legs and let it sit for five or so minutes. Then shower and the hair rinses off."

"How'd you figure that out?"

"One of the officers sprayed it on his arm. It's just a guess at this point. We'll know for sure after the lab does testing."

"Doesn't Hair-B-Gone smell gross?" I ask.

"You can get it scented. And the hair spritz probably wasn't straight Hair-B-Gone, just cut with it. Otherwise, those women would be bald."

Ack. Eek. Ike. "Anyone could buy Hair-B-Gone."

"Certainly. Will could."

I tell her why I think we were totally on the wrong track with Will. "I wanna get back to the tapes. There's gotta be something on them. Especially because Josh and Nick were filming from different angles."

"Where's Grandma?" Mom asks.

"She went home. She said she needed to spend some time with her birds and think over the whole experience."

"How upset was she?"

"Not as upset as I was expecting," I say. "But, uh, I'm sure Sam's spot as her fave is pretty safe."

"Grandma doesn't love Sam any more than she loves you. It's just a different kind of relationship."

"Yeah, well, he didn't just talk her into a public hair-loss ordeal."

"It'll be fine."

"Mom"—my throat goes all tight—"Mrs. Howard said I ruined everything."

She blows out a long breath. "Let's take care of this case first, and then we'll worry about Mrs. Howard and the foreign Academy."

"I feel horrible." Tears prick at my eyes. "I wrecked things for a lot of people and ghosts."

Someone bangs on the stall door. "Hurry up!"

"But if we solve this case, you'll have saved Lacey's business and kept a lot of customers safe."

My mother has a way of always making me feel better.

There's more insistent pounding on the door. "Don't be a selfish jerk. Go talk on your phone somewhere else. This is a *public* restroom."

"I'm heading over to the station," Mom says. "I'll catch up with you later."

"Thanks, Mom. I really mean it."

"I know, pumpkin."

And I know she really is distressed about the foreign Academy position going up in smoke. But my mother? She's so not a drama queen. Especially during an ongoing investigation.

"Sherry?" Junie calls out. "Are you okay?"

"That your friend hogging the stall?" a girl snarls. "Tell her to get out."

I open the door. "Sorry," I say to the scowling girl on the other side. "Avoid the chicken teriyaki bowl."

"Amber just texted," Junie says. "The police think it was Hair-B-Gone."

I nod. "My mom just told me." Yay Amber for texting. Now I don't have to come up with an explanation for how I know about the Hair-B-Gone. "I'm dying to watch the tapes."

We sprint back to the food court.

Nick sits, holding the camera, while the rest of us huddle over him, jostling to see the small playback screen.

"What're we looking for?" Josh asks.

"Anything, anybody," I say. "Just point out even the smallest thing that strikes you as odd."

When the tape ends, Junie says, "I didn't see anything weird. Did anyone?"

Nothing but head shakes.

I break into a cold sweat. There has to be a clue on the tapes.

Nick pops in Josh's tape.

I'm staring so hard my eyes are watering. It's like I don't want to blink in case I miss the one little something that turns into the one big something.

And then I spot it!

chapter
thirty-three

I clap and spin in a circle. "That's it! That's it. I saw it!"

"What?" Junie says. "What did you see?"

Josh squeezes my shoulder.

"Way to go, Sherry," Nick says.

"Give me the camera, Nick, and I'll show you guys." I reach for the equipment. I hit Rewind, then Play; then I slow it all down.

Lacey lifts the brush and sets it on Grandma's hair. She drags downward. The camera follows the hair as it plops to the ground. And then Josh, my beautiful, wonderful Josh, had the presence of mind to scan the audience.

Everyone's eyes are focused in the same direction. Everyone's mouth hits the ground.

One person smiles.

"Look at her," I point at the screen. "Just look at her."

"Crystal!" Junie says, stunned.

Crystal leans forward. Probably to get a better view. A bright yellow bottle begins to slide from her pocket. She shoves it back in.

"Hair-B-Gone," I say.

"We never even suspected her." Junie slaps her forehead in frustration.

"When do you think she messed with the hair spritz?" Nick asks.

"This morning, while she was helping Amber get ready for Fantabulous You!, Amber was rushing all over the place, doing a zillion things," I answer. "For sure, she left Crystal alone. She totally trusts Crystal. So does Lacey."

"I guess Naked Makeup, with help from Amber, was luring away Crystal's clients." Junie snaps her fingers. "And remember her talking about getting a huge promotion to Montreal if she kept her sales up? Amber said it was her dream job."

"And she saw that her sales were dipping all of a sudden, so she must've decided to take control of the situation and shut down Naked Makeup." Nick leans over and turns off the camera. "Sherry, we'll make a DVD for you with all the material from both cameras."

"Thanks, Nick." Who knew he could be so helpful.

"This isn't enough to go to the cops with, right?" Josh takes a bite of his sandwich.

"Not even close." I sip from Josh's Sprite.

"We need to find out where Crystal got the Hair-B-Gone," Junie says. "Because there's a definite pattern to how she's procuring contaminants. And the pattern is they're all from nearby."

Junie is crazy for patterns. And I'm starting to see how useful they are.

"She could easily have gotten habanero peppers from Will's kiosk for the lip gloss," Nick says.

"And for the night cream with the extra papaya acid? Crystal's the queen of face peels. Maybe she just grabbed something from her own makeup counter," I say.

"Probably all she did was yank up a couple of prickly pear cactus plants from the mall garden and shove spines in some of the hand cream bottles." Josh takes another bite.

"For the sake of argument"—Junie straightens her glasses—"let's assume the Hair-B-Gone comes from nearby. The closest place is the drugstore on the second level."

"We can go talk to the cashiers." Nick jumps up.

"Everyone who works at the mall knows everyone else who works here."

"And she wears a lot of jewelry," I say, "which makes her easy to recognize."

"The mall security cameras might've picked her up entering or exiting the drugstore. And it'll be time-stamped." Josh rolls up the paper that wrapped his sandwich and lobs it into the nearest trash can. "I talked to the security guys yesterday about doing a segment for *Revealing Phoenix*. They were way cool and helpful. Plus, a couple of them played polo in high school, and we really connected. I'll go back and talk with them some more. I bet they let me watch a bunch of their tapes. Who knows what got caught on those."

Head cocked, I smile at my three friends. "You guys are the best. We're gonna nail her. Crystal doesn't stand a chance against us." I flutter my fingers in the air. "I'm going after fingerprints. That bottle of Hair-B-Gone is somewhere. Quite possibly in the trash can at the kiosk. She probably got all her contaminants at the mall. I bet she leaves her trash here too. Crystal's a lazy crook. And that really works in our favor.

"We'll keep in touch with our cells." I stand. "Let's go find some hard evidence!"

* * *

Adrenaline rushes through me, filling me with extra energy and speed. I jog toward the Naked Makeup kiosk and its cute pink + butterflies trash can.

Mr. Peabody ordered one of his security guys to stand guard, but Lacey always leaves the trash can in the same place. So I figure I'll just skip around there, fake-drop an earring, and root in the trash while fake-hunting for the earring.

I'm especially optimistic because I'm remembering Amber, Lacey and Crystal complaining about the trash service at the mall and how there's never any pickup.

When I get to the kiosk, the security guard's leaning against an end and texting with one hand. He looks about sixteen. He barely even blinks as I skip close. Unfortunately, he's right by the trash can, but I think I can handle the situation.

I pull out my phone and start chatting with nobody.

"He is so not my type." I skip past the guard. "Besides which, he's my older brother's best friend's teacher's brother's kid. Even if he asks, I am so not going to the dance with him. Think how embarrassing it would be for everyone if we started dating and then broke up. I can't do that to my family."

The security guard shoots me a "could you be more stupid" look.

Good. He'll pay less attention to a moron.

I drop to my knees by the trash can and start feeling around the floor with my free hand.

"Excuse me," he says. "You need to move along. No one's allowed here."

"My earring just fell out. It was a gift from my fifth-grade Christmas party. Which means sentimental value, if you're wondering. It's the only school souvenir I have from that year."

"Move along."

Still slapping the floor, I say into the phone, "No, I'm not talking to you. It's this security guy." I look at his badge. "His name's Adam. And, yeah, he's cute."

"I can hear you. I'm standing right here." Adam waves.

I point to my phone and put my index finger against my lips. "I'm pretty sure he finds me cute too. He won't stop talking to me."

"No, I don't." He frowns. "I don't find you cute at all. Anyway, aren't you, like, in middle school?"

"Now he's judging me." I'm about two inches from the trash. "No, I'm not going to cry." I gulp loudly. "Seriously, I'm fine."

Adam throws his arms up in despair and stomps to the other end of the kiosk.

In a flash, I tip the trash can on its side and peek in. Empty!

I hop up, drop my phone in my purse and take off

running to the department store. There's a good chance Crystal wouldn't be dumb enough to toss the Hair-B-Gone in Lacey's trash. She probably believes no one will ever suspect her in a million years. Which means no one would ever think to check the trash at her counter.

No one except me!

I'm dashing along, cursing under my breath. Why oh why did the janitors choose today to actually empty the trash cans? I cross my fingers, hoping they went for a break and never emptied Crystal's trash.

At the department store, I screech to a halt. Crystal's over at Suze's counter, showing a customer lash curlers.

For the second time in ten minutes, I drop to the floor. Catlike, I crawl next to Crystal's display case and slink around the corner. I keep low and out of sight. It's my pounding heart that might give me away.

I sneak behind the counter, reach into the trash.

Empty!

Foiled again!

I retrace my steps, crawling backward until I'm in the shoe department. I pull myself to my feet and dust off my knees.

The good news: Crystal didn't spot me.

The bad news: My next stop will be the nearest Dumpster.

I slide the bolt, releasing the Dumpster lid. Then, with two hands, I heave it back and open.

I'm not actually climbing in the Dumpster. The Hair-B-Gone bottle must be in a trash bag very recently chucked in here. I'll just walk my fingers along the top bags and . . . I can't feel any bags. Everything's too far down.

Yikes! I'm going in.

I curl my fingers around the lip of the Dumpster opening. My beautiful oversized denim purse slips off my shoulder, down my arm and dangles from my wrist, clunking against my hip. I let it drop to the asphalt. Why subject this adorable accessory to the horrors of a Dumpster? Probably it would soak up the trashy smell and attract loud, meowing alley cats for months to come. No, my purse does not need to face humiliation. Bad enough that I'm sacrificing my plaid shorts and scoop-neck top.

Sherry Holmes Baldwin, Dumpster Diver.

A quick check around. No witnesses. The Dumpster's way at the end of the parking lot. There's not a car around.

One. Two. Three.

I haul myself up, throw a leg over the edge, plug my

nose and tumble in. I land on my back. On a bed of bumpy, chunky plastic trash bags. I listen carefully. Nothing. Phew. No rats.

The inside of the Dumpster is rusty. And stinky. But not very full.

This is the absolute grossest thing I have ever done in my entire life. By far. The sooner I get out of here, the better.

I unplug my nose and breathe through my mouth. I'll be faster with two free hands. I start squeezing bags from the outside, feeling for a bottle shape.

I get lucky. I happen upon a trash bag loaded with bottle shapes. I tear it open. Pay dirt! It's full of cosmetic products. From the department store.

And there in the middle, not even attempting to hide from me, is a sunshine yellow bottle of Hair-B-Gone.

How to pick it up without destroying fingerprints?

Using the hem of my T-shirt as a rag, I carefully hold the bottom of the bottle. I don't want to smudge any of Crystal's precious prints.

Unfortunately, climbing out of a Dumpster is harder than climbing in. I'm trying to balance, one-handed, on a slippery bed of bags crammed with irregular shapes. Not working. I need both hands to pull myself up to the lip.

I drop the bottle of Hair-B-Gone outside the Dumpster. It thuds on the ground.

I crouch down low, ready to spring up like a tiger
and hoist myself out of the land of stink.
Just as I'm uncoiling, the lid slams shut.
The world goes dark.
The bolt rasps.
I'm trapped.

chapter
thirty-four

"**H**elp! Help!" I yell. "I'm in here!"

Nothing.

I pound on the sides, scraping my knuckles.

Nothing.

I pound and yell.

Still nothing.

I talk to myself. "Sherry, do not panic. Yes, you are trapped in a rusty, smelly, dark Dumpster where no one hears your pounding and screaming. But, think, think, think—there must be a way out."

My mom!

The Ziploc bag of espresso coffee beans is in my purse. And I see my purse slipping and sliding down my arm to a safe haven on the ground, near the Dumpster. I can't call my mother.

My friends!

I reach into my jeans pocket for my phone. Not there. And then I remember slipping my phone in my purse after I checked the trash at the kiosk. I can't call my friends.

The situation is dire.

Sitting in the pitch black on lumpy, stinky trash bags, I hunch over and grab my knees. And start to cry.

Then I cry harder, because the situation is beyond dire. The Dumpster isn't even half full. I don't hear the wheels of a cart rolling along the parking lot pavement. It could be days before a janitor stops by with the next load of trash.

Then I cry some more because the situation is beyond beyond dire. Do I really think an over-enthusiastic mall janitor who likes closed lids happened by and accidentally locked me in the Dumpster?

No, this is the work of Crystal!

She must've spotted me checking her trash. She figured out I was on to her and followed me to the Dumpster. Even worse, she probably discovered the bright yellow bottle of Hair-B-Gone on the ground. Which means she has the evidence.

Not only have I botched the makeup mystery, I've let down loads of people and ghosts. My mom, the entire Academy, the entire mysterious foreign Academy, people all over the world who will be way less safe because of me.

I've never felt this low before. Ever.

Finally, even I run out of tears. I wipe under my eyes with the back of my hand. I sniff loudly.

Weirdly, a good cry clears my head. And this is what I come up with.

I gotta save myself.

I feel around in the dark for something to bang the sides and the lid with. Something that will make a louder noise than my voice.

And I find it. A plank of wood.

I grasp the wood and start swinging and connecting with metal. The metal sides, the metal lid. It's loud. It's echoey. It's probably damaging my hearing.

But I keep on swinging. Even when my arms feel like they're going to tear loose from their sockets. Even when my muscles are screaming with fatigue. I'm swinging for my mom. I'm swinging for Lacey. I'm swinging for freedom everywhere.

"Sherry!"

"Nick?"

"I found her!" Nick yells. "I found her!"

The bolt creaks across. The lid pops open. Sunlight floods in, blinding me.

I stand. With two very weary arms, I pull myself up and peer over the edge:

Josh, Junie, Nick and Adam, the security guard.

Adam takes a step back, like I'm one of America's Most Wanted. "You?"

My dad and The Ruler made all the usual grown-up noises about how I took risks and how I could've been really hurt and yada, yada, yada. But, basically, they're super proud of me.

I'm all showered and dressed in clean clothes and kicking it on our backyard patio with Josh, Junie, Nick and Brianna. Brianna's thrilled that she had an afternoon appointment for Fantabulous You! because, of course, it was canceled. Which means she has all her hair. The girls are spending the night.

Sam's watering. The Ruler's releasing ladybugs into the tomato plants. Grandma's wandering around the garden with them, touching her head from time to time, where she's wound a tie-dyed kerchief. On Monday, she's getting together with Amber, who promised to work on her with hair extensions and weaves. For now, anyway, Grandma seems pretty okay with the multicolored kerchief thing she's got going. My dad's messing with the barbecue, getting ready to grill up a bunch of burgers and tofu something-or-other.

Earlier, we explained everything to the police and

to the mall manager. Lacey's back in business. Crystal's in deep trouble. No one knows yet what she'll be charged with, but it could be as serious as aggravated assault, meaning she tried to hurt people on purpose.

Now we're going over the details and filling in Brianna.

"I'll never forget sitting in the security office and watching those cameras when, all of sudden, Crystal jogs into the mall, hauling Sherry's purse." Josh turns his deep blue eyes on me. "Very freaky." He rubs my shoulder. "And then I called Sherry's cell, and Crystal reached into that huge purse, feeling around, trying to find it." Josh grabs my hand under the table. "I had no idea where Sherry was."

"Oooh." Brianna gives a little shake. "Scary."

Oooh. And how romantic to hear how worried Josh was about me.

"That's when Nick and I showed up." Junie scoops up a few chips. "We'd been to the drugstore and learned that Crystal bought the Hair-B-Gone there. I phoned Sherry's cell, but she didn't answer. So we raced to security to see Josh, hoping he knew what was up."

"I was really impressed with the mall security." Nick pops the tab on a can of a Coke. "The guy watching the cameras with Josh didn't even hesitate, but immediately called for backup. He watched where Crystal went via the cameras and kept in constant contact with the security guy trying to pick her up." He sips. "And he involved the mall manager right away."

"My favorite part was calling your phone over and over." Junie giggles. "Crystal never could find it in your ginormous purse. It was driving her nuts."

"So the security guy followed the sounds of 'You're the One,' by the Boyfriends, right to her." I laugh.

"Crystal crumbled in two seconds and told the security guy she'd locked Sherry in a Dumpster," Josh says.

"Apparently, Crystal kept running on at the mouth. It was like once she admitted what she'd done"— Nick passes his Coke to Junie—"she couldn't stop the flow. Good thing the mall manager showed up quickly, so he could make sense of what was going on."

Josh looks at me. "How do you know Adam, the security guy that caught Crystal? When you jumped out of the Dumpster, he totally recognized you."

My face goes hot. "I was checking Lacey's trash, and he was kind of giving me a hard time because he wasn't allowed to let anyone hang around there. And I was, uh, giving him a hard time back."

We go quiet, just chilling. Solving the mystery together created a bond, and we're all sitting there remembering the investigation in our own way. Even

Brianna can relate, because she passed on info about the Janes.

"How about some Ping-Pong?" Josh squeezes my hand, then lets go and stands. "Sherry and I'll take on anybody."

"Don't expect much from me. My arms are still super sore from whacking the Dumpster with the board." But I head into the shed to grab paddles and balls.

A coffee smell whooshes in next to me.

"Mom!"

"Congratulations, Sherry. You solved another mystery."

"How are you? What's going to happen? Are you in trouble?"

"According to Mrs. Howard, I am. I won't know the details till I get called in for a meeting."

"I'm really sorry, Mom. I ruined your chances with the foreign Academy."

"I wouldn't change how I handled things. Except I wish I'd been in on the mystery sooner. Anyway, I came by to make sure the investigation is all wrapped up for you."

"Well"—I twirl my hair around my finger—"I get the motive about Crystal wanting to shut down Naked Makeup so she'd get her customers back and rock her sales and land the Montreal job."

"Right," Mom says.

"Lacey and Amber never questioned why she hung around the kiosk. They considered her a good friend." I pick up paddles and balls. "She had loads of opportunity."

"You identified all the contaminants," Mom says.

"And she got hold of them easily." I shove Ping-Pong balls in my shorts pocket.

"Exactly," my mom says. "The active ingredient in the chili pepper is capsicum. I have a little extra info on the time-release papaya acid. Nite Sprite Creme normally contains two percent acid, which is low enough that you can leave it on all night. Crystal boosted it up to twenty percent, which should only be left on for a matter of minutes. She added in time-release beads filled with extra papaya acid."

"She used the time-release acid so we'd leave it on too long?"

"Yes. She assumed the burning and itchiness would eventually wake the user up, but not until the acid had done some skin damage."

Sam powers into the shed. "Where's the Ping-Pong stuff? Brianna said she'd be my partner." His eyes are bright.

I pass him the equipment.

He turns to leave, then freezes. "Remember when I was telling you how it sometimes feels like Mom's here and watching over us?"

Goose bumps pop up on my arms. "Yeah."

257

Sam peers around the shed. "I have that feeling right now. Do you?"

"Yeah." Goose bumps pop up on top of my goose bumps.

"I love that feeling." He waves a paddle at me. "Brianna and me will own you and Josh." He runs out.

"Sam senses me." Mom's voice catches.

The barbecue has cooled down. The backyard is tidied up. The guys and Grandma have left. Our house is quiet.

Except for me, Junie and Brianna. We're sitting cross-legged on sleeping bags in the middle of my room. We are totally wide awake and looking for fun.

"Wanna make popcorn and watch scary movies?" I ask.

Brianna's playing with her hair, holding it up high in a ponytail, then letting it swish loose. "I'm not in the mood for scary. A chick flick maybe."

"I know what I'm never doing." Junie smoothes out her pillow. "Night cream." She leans back. "I'm not risking an experience like that again."

Brianna and I sigh.

"Totally understandable," Brianna says. "Even though, thanks to you guys, Naked Makeup is safe, you don't want to take chances with your face. I mean, you only have one."

Junie places her hands on her cheeks as if to protect them. "You got it." She wrinkles her nose to push up her glasses. "That's a whole area of makeup that's over for us now."

The three of us blow out a long, deep breath. Then we sit quietly, hugging our knees, in the bluish glow of the aquarium light and contemplate this sad, sad fact.

"Unless," I say slowly, "we make our own cream. And we only put in super healthy and natural ingredients."

"And mix it up ourselves," Brianna says quickly.

Junie's got her phone open and logs on to Google faster than you can say "Nite Sprite Creme." "Does The Ruler have old-fashioned oats and plain yogurt?" she asks.

I jump up. "Definitely!"

We tiptoe down the stairs, along the hall and into the kitchen. Brianna's hunting for yogurt in the fridge, Junie's getting down a mixing bowl, and I'm in the pantry, scrounging for oats.

"Sherry!" Brianna calls. "There's a bird pecking at the window by the sink. He's pecking hard enough to crack the glass."

Junie pokes her head into the pantry. "It's your grandfather," she whispers.

I plunk the container of oats on the counter, then unlock the porch door.

Brianna's on my heels. "I'll help you get rid of him."

"I'm good, Bri." I crack the door so that only I can squeeze through. "This happens all the time."

"There are some very weird things about your life, Sherry." Shaking her head, she wanders over to Junie and the ingredients.

I step onto the back porch.

With a raggedy flutter, Grandpa swoops around the corner, setting off the motion light. He hovers in the air by my head. He squawks, "Good job, Sherry."

Or he might've squawked, "You're a blob, Sherry." But I decide to assume it's the compliment. "Thanks, Grandpa."

"Dairy Queen. Tomorrow. Ten a.m."

Yikes.

chapter
thirty-five

I arrive early at Dairy Queen.

Unlike my last visit, the place is pretty empty. I use the restroom to prepare for my trip across the threshold with the regular stuff: sunglasses, bike helmet, aluminum foil.

Before leaving the house, I tossed an extra item into my backpack. Tape. For extra arm and leg coverage, I tape down the foil.

I pull open the Employees Only door and step through the Portal of Pain. It's not as difficult to cross this time. Maybe because I'm better protected. Maybe because I'm early, it's not turned on full force. Maybe I'm so depressed about how my actions have messed up things for so many people and ghosts that the pain is the same, but I'm not feeling it.

Whatev. I'm in the Academy of Spirits. Alone. I yank off my helmet and sunglasses and shove them in my backpack. Then I slump down on the bench.

No Oreo Cookies Blizzard. Not that I was really expecting one. But it would've been nice.

I sit there, slouched over and sad. I wonder what's going to happen to my mother. She certainly won't get picked up for an assignment by the persnickety foreign Academy. All because I stubbornly went ahead with an investigation. I feel horrible.

My eyes fill with tears.

The problem is that I don't think I could've changed the choices I made. Which makes it all even worse. But I wanted to help Lacey. And I wanted to catch the person who tampered with the makeup and harmed me and Brianna and especially Junie.

The tears spill over and trickle down my cheeks. My nose starts running. I'm not a pretty crier.

And then I smell it. That strange smell from yesterday at the mall. The smell of the ghost from the foreign Academy.

Yikes. I cannot even cry without being spied on.

The smell gets closer. The ghost is across the table from me. He's completely invisible. I can't see even a vague outline.

Of course, he doesn't realize I'm aware of his presence.

We sit, in silence.

Then I start getting mad. He's spying on me. Plus, he's pulling the plug on my mom's happiness all because I solved a makeup mystery.

"I know you're there," I say.

"What? How do you know this?" He speaks with a foreign accent, but not one I can identify.

"I can smell you."

"This wasn't in your file."

"Because Mrs. Howard doesn't know."

He laughs, long and loud. "You didn't tell her on purpose? So when she's secretly checking on you, it's not a secret for you."

"Bingo."

He laughs again. "You are full of surprises, Sherry Holmes Baldwin."

"Look, you shouldn't blame my mother for what I did. Mrs. Howard warned me not to solve the mystery, but I just did it anyway. That's my problem. My mom was so thrilled learning animal mind control for you guys. Please don't take that away from her. Just because of me." Embarrassingly, I'm crying again. Big rivers of tears splash down my face.

A box of Kleenex slides through the wall and settles on the table.

I pluck out a few and blow my nose.

He waits until I calm down. "What makes you think you've done anything wrong?"

"Mrs. Howard told me I ruined everything."

"Ah, Mrs. Howard . . ."

An Oreo Cookies Blizzard materializes in front of me. "How did you know? Oh, my file."

"Yes. Now, eat up and let me tell you a little about our Academy."

I scoop up a bite. I'm always amazed at how hungry crying makes me.

"We are an Academy that has been around for a long, long time. Which means we've had centuries to determine which characteristics in our agents aid in our struggle to protect humans." He pauses. "Above all, we value loyalty and creativity. Your mother has these in abundance. Anyone who would defy Mrs. Howard's rules to help her daughter is exactly the kind of individual we're looking for. The manner in which your mother relates to animals indicates someone who clearly thinks outside the box." He pauses again. "And, Sherry, you possess the same admirable traits."

"But Mrs. Howard said—"

"You must let this Mrs. Howard go. She doesn't have a creative bone in her body. Actually, she doesn't have a bone at all in her body." He snorts.

He reminds me of my dad with his bad jokes.

"You'll offer my mother the job?"

"Without a doubt."

"How about me?"

"We'd like to keep that door open. At the moment, we don't have an assignment that fits your talents. But in the future? Perhaps."

"Who are you? What country are you from? What is that smell?"

"All in good time, my curious friend." He laughs again. "Besides the Kleenex and the Blizzard, is there anything else I can do for you?

"I want my mom."

"I presume we're speaking of Real Time?"

"Please."

"Is there a particular Blizzard your mother would enjoy?"

"She'd love a coffee. Black."

The smell moves up above me. "While I find her, why don't you catch up on the WWWD headlines."

The plasma screen appears on the wall.

"You have a half hour together, Sherry."

A half hour? I didn't even know that was possible! I want to dance around the room. And sing and shout. A half hour! And I was hoping for five minutes.

The screen shimmers. Headlines appear and begin scrolling.

Teen Girl Does It Again!

Makeup Is Safe in Phoenix

Living Teen Solves Mystery Alone

What's Next for the Mother-
Daughter Duo?

Sherry Holmes Baldwin
Cracks the Case

The screen dims and disappears. Another Oreo
Cookies Blizzard and a large coffee exit from the wall
and travel to the table.

There's a rush of French-roast-scented air.

And then she's here.

My mother is standing next to the table.

She looks exactly the same as she did the day she
died. Right down to the haircut she needed, but
never got. Her dark curls hang below her chin. Her
brown eyes watch me with pride. She smiles, big and
wide, just like I remember. "Sherry!"

All crinkly sounds from the aluminum foil, I jump
up from the table. And run into her arms.

It's almost too much to grasp. I'm hugging my
mother. I'm actually hugging her. And touching her.
And feeling her. My mother, who died two years ago.
My chest feels like it will burst open.

I step back. "Mom, am I taller than you?"

"Absolutely not. You're not passing me by at the age of thirteen."

"Uh, I think I am. I'm a little over five feet one." We're both short.

We stand back-to-back. I press my palm on the top of our heads. "I so am taller than you. By a smidgen. But a smidgen counts."

Eventually, we sit. My legs stretched out to the bench across from me and my feet resting next to her, I dig into my Blizzard.

Mom pries off her coffee lid and sips carefully from the edge. Her lips leave behind an imprint of Perfectly Plum, her fave lipstick.

Her eyes widen with excitement. "Let's do our nails."

My mother worked too much and was gone from home a lot. She definitely missed some major maternal moments. But something we've always shared is a love of painted nails.

I nod at the perfect suggestion. "But how?"

The question barely escapes my mouth when a tray of polish and emery boards and other manicure junk materializes from the wall. I so need a generous wall like this in my room!

The tray slides to a stop by my mom's elbow. She chooses an emery board. I stick out my arms. She takes my right hand in hers and starts filing.

My heart kind of stops. I'd forgotten little things, like how quickly she shapes my nails and how she only files in one direction. And how her touch is soft but sure.

"Will I remember this time we're spending together?" I ask.

My mom sets down the emery board and looks at me. "You shouldn't. Humans don't remember Real Time. But you've surprised the Academy over and over." She pushes the tray toward me. "Bottom line—we don't really know."

"I hope I do." I pick out a teal polish, Summer Breeze, shake it, then pass it to her. "Did the foreign ghost dude tell you they're giving you the assignment?"

Mom grins. "He did. I can't wait to get started. And it sounds like, down the road, they'll have something for the two of us."

"So what country is he from?"

"He wouldn't tell me." She paints a blue stripe down the middle of my thumbnail from base to tip.

"What's his name?" With my free hand, I scoop up some Blizzard on my spoon. "Maybe we could figure out his nationality from that."

"I don't know." She finishes by dragging the pad of her index finger across the edge of my nail, her fail-proof method to prevent chipping.

"He smells weird," I say. "An herb or a spice that's new to me."

"Working for their organization will be interesting. Very different from here. Fewer guidelines, but somehow I think they'll expect more." Mom's eyes twinkle while she talks shop.

This used to bug me big-time when she was alive. How into work she'd get until it was almost like I didn't exist. But it doesn't feel like that now. Strange as it sounds, our relationship is more balanced now that she's a ghost.

"How's French going?" Mom asks.

"That is one tough language." I shake my head. "Hard to believe there's an entire country that communicates with it. I feel bad for them."

"What's your grade?"

"C. But I think I'll raise it to a B with the French cultural project we're doing now." I tell her how everyone's typing up a report on the computer. "But not me. I'm bringing in Sam's wagon. And pretending it's a French restaurant kiosk. Paula's getting me croissants and cold potato soup and bottles of water. And then everyone will order in French. And I have little bills I designed and printed on the computer. I even made a poster that shows what I serve. Madame Blanchard will totally love it."

Mom glues five small sparkly rhinestones in a half-moon on my ring finger. It's our signature design. Each stone stands for a word: I. Love. You. Very. Much.

When my nails on both hands are dry, I say, "Hey,

let me show you what Sam gave me. I've been carrying it around with me." I reach into the front pocket of my backpack. "He's on this kick of giving gifts for no reason." I pull out the tiny frame.

Mom takes it from me. "Oh. It's the last photo of the three of us together." She pats her heart. "He's such a sensitive little guy." She examines the photo. "You remember this Saturday trip out to the desert. On the day the desert flowers bloomed. Every year, we kept missing them. But that time, we made it, and it turned out to be such a letdown."

"Well, yeah. There were like three blooming flowers. Big whoop." I roll my eyes. "But we still had fun. Especially when we stopped for huge milk shakes."

We keep on chatting, mostly about ordinary stuff. Because that's what daily life is all about. And Real Time feels like a slice of life. I paint Mom's nails a muted pink. She does the half-moon design.

Our cups and the tray skim along the tabletop and through the wall.

A buzzer sounds.

"How much time do we have left?" My pulse races. I don't want this to ever be over.

"Thirty seconds."

I stare at her, memorizing her face.

"We'll do this again." My mother hooks my hair around my ears, then leans across the table and kisses my forehead.

We stand for a last hug, and I hold on tight, as if there's even a chance that'll prevent her from disappearing.

"Sherry, you're the best daughter a mother could hope for." She squeezes me hard. "I'm so proud of you."

Then, *poof*, she's gone. Not just invisible, but gone.

All alone, I gaze around the small back room of Dairy Queen, taking in the white walls that need a coat of paint, the empty table, my backpack on the floor.

I glance down at my nails, the rhinestones winking in the fluorescent light. I. Love. You. Very. Much.

I remember. Every single detail.

You so don't want to
miss Barrie Summy's
next book

i so
don't do
famous

Coming in 2011!

Barrie Summy grew up in Canada with beaucoup de books, butter tarts, and Bonne Bell makeup. She lives in California with her husband, their four children, two veiled chameleons, and a dog named Dorothy. Barrie is hard at work on her next book. Visit her at www.barriesummy.com.